ROUGH GHOST LOVER

A SEXY GHOST STORY

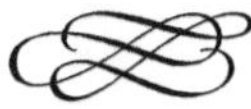

CASSIE ALEXANDER

CASKARA PRESS

I thought I had everything: a devoted husband, and a magnificent new house for us to start a family in.

But the house had secrets. The former owner, whose stern portrait hangs in the library -- swear I can feel him watching me. Touching me. Wanting me.

I could convince myself it was all in my mind until I found out my husband cheated on me...but now, all bets are off.

Rough Ghost Lover is a sizzling and sexy horror novel. It does not have an HEA (because sleeping with ghosts, while sexy, is bad!)

For more about Cassie's other books, sneak peeks at works in progress, playlists, and cat photos, sign up for her mailing list by clicking on the word HERE or go to http://www.cassiealexander. com/roughghost-news.

Thanks! — CA

CHAPTER 1

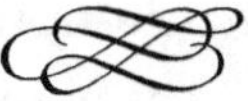

Daphne stood on the cool white tile of her new entry hall, looking up at her husband with distress. "But we just got here—"

"I know, pet, I know," Richard said, but he didn't set his briefcase down.

"And there's so much unpacking to do—I don't even know where everything goes." Boxes were piled everywhere, their belongings and those the house's prior occupants had left behind. She didn't even know how many rooms their new home had, it was immense—and how could it feel like a home to her, if Richard left her alone their first night there?

"You'll put it all right. You always do. I'll be back before you know it." He reached out and gently held her chin. "It's just a week."

"And then?"

"And then I'll come back and you and I can spend the rest of our lives together."

"You always say that. And it's never just a week." She stared at him, refusing to back down for once. They'd bought this place to have a child in, and children didn't just make themselves.

The driver idling outside cleared his throat—Richard had a flight to catch. "This time I promise," he said, turning to leave.

"That's what you said last time," she said quietly to herself, watching him go.

DAPHNE SAT down on the wide stairs leading to the second floor. It was always like this with Richard—in the battle between her and his work, work won. She'd known it going into their relationship. It'd been fine when they'd been nearer civilization—she'd gone to movies, bookstores, lunches. But now that he'd moved her here, miles away from the nearest town, with the nearest city far past that—her sense of abandonment was overwhelming. The size of the house he'd bought her only made it worse. It was too big, too easy to imagine that the house was like a mouth, swallowing her alive.

She'd begged him not to buy it, but he'd been enchanted the moment he'd stepped on the grounds. Something here had intoxicated him, even though they would never own enough things to fill it up, that half the rooms would be gathering dust, unused. It'd given him some old world vision of himself as the lord of a manor, and once the grandeur had gotten hold of him, there'd been no way to shake it loose.

No matter that she couldn't see herself out here, in this massive place, completely alone. Or rather, awkwardly not alone. There were servants—*servants!*—and Daphne found that distasteful. But there was no way to manage a home this big without them. The real estate agent had called some of the old owner's employees back and only the fact that she and Richard were paying them handsomely combined with the fact that she planned to require as little from them as possible made it okay.

Of course, now they were nowhere to be found, and she didn't know how to call for them. Daphne imagined herself wandering the halls, shouting like a madwoman or wildly ringing bells. Perhaps she could ask them to listen for whistles, like little Von Trapps.

"Mrs. Vance?"

She couldn't see who asked, but she jumped to standing. She didn't want anyone else to see her despairing on the stair.

"Sorry to startle you, Ma'am." An elderly man in a black suit bowed deeply. She knew his name was Arthur. Could she call him that? Or was there some foolish title she ought to be using instead?

"No. It's okay." Both of their voices echoed in the hallway, uncomfortably loud.

"I came to ask what time you wanted Mrs. Dudley to serve dinner."

Servants, cooking for her—it was preposterous! But they were getting paid, and she didn't even know where the kitchen was yet—or a grocery store. "Seven?" she guessed, hoping he'd agree.

"Very good." He gave her a precise nod. "We've unpacked the kitchen—which room would you like us to work on next?"

She would need a place to sleep tonight, but couldn't stomach the thought of strangers rummaging through her intimate things. "I'll work on the bedroom—maybe you can work on the library? That's if you have the time."

"Of course, Ma'am. I'll just let Mrs. Dudley know about dinner." He nodded again, and Daphne turned. The bedrooms were all upstairs. She walked up three steps and felt something like a warm hand caress the back of her thigh beneath her skirt.

"Arthur!" she protested, whirling.

"Ma'am?" The servant reappeared, trotting back into view from down the hall. "Did you need something?"

Daphne put her hand to her mouth in horror, and felt a rising flush of shame—he was going to think she was one of those people, the kind who shouted. "No—my ankle twisted," she pointed at her foot, quickly lying. "I thought I was going to fall."

"I see," he said, in the same tone of voice he used for everything apparently, neither frustrated nor surprised. "I can bring tea or coffee to you in a bit, if you'd like. Mrs. Dudley's got bad knees, she can't handle stairs anymore."

"Tea, please. Thank you," she said, sheepishly.

"If I may, Ma'am," he said after waiting half-a-second more. She nodded to encourage him to continue. "Moving is stressful, and moving into a magnificent house doubly so. Rome was not built in a day, and neither was it unpacked in one."

She broke into a soft smile. "Thank you, Arthur."

"You're welcome, Ma'am," he said, and bowed curtly before going back the way he'd come.

DAPHNE SPENT the whole afternoon drinking tea and unpacking boxes. The bedroom she and Richard had picked out had a commanding view of the gardens and two closets of roughly equal size. She decided to take the one nearer the bed that had a mirror set inside the door.

They'd chosen it because it was the only room that didn't have the belongings of prior occupants inside it—the home's past owners had left behind massive pieces of handmade-looking furniture and interesting yet difficult to understand art. Statues of angels or demons—the creatures in them were winged and striving—perched at the top of both of the stairs, as if watching who came up, and occupied corners in many of the rooms.

But the bedroom was her domain alone, and the repetitive work of opening boxes, exposing the contents, and deciding what went where and how—it didn't clear her depression but it did calm her. Keeping busy always did.

What would she do when she ran out of boxes though?

There was a polite knock at the door and she went to open it. For a foolish second she hoped it was Richard, returned to his senses and to her, but instead it was only Arthur again, as it had been all afternoon.

"It's seven, Ma'am. We were going to wait, but then we realized you might not have unpacked a clock yet."

"Thank you, Arthur." Her cell phone told the time, but not much more, they were so far from civilization they had to use landlines. "I am hungry."

He bowed and prepared to exit the room, as if to give her privacy. "Wait!"

"Yes?" he paused in the doorway.

"I don't know where the dining room is. Can you take me?"

He smiled at her. "Of course," he said, and led the way.

It hadn't occurred to her to shower or change before dinner—this was her house, after all—but the dining room that Arthur took her to was glamorous. Seeing a reflection of herself in a mirror on the way there, looking wan and exhausted, only made her feel more out of place. The last people who'd eaten here had surely been gracious-types—she could see the marks on the walls where their vast portraits must have hung, forefathers and foxhounds looking down on whomever stole the last bite of cake. Mrs. Dudley's dinner setting took up only one corner of the massive oaken table, left behind by the former owner's family, who probably hadn't been able to think of a way to dismantle it to get it out the door.

Daphne sat down and realized they were using her mother's china, something she, cooking for only herself and Richard, had never done. She was stroking a flower painted on the plate's edge when the first course arrived.

She hadn't been close to her mother, but her mother had kept her nearby, through a combination of guilt and necessity, as her health took precipitous turns. Daphne'd been the only one able to care for her, to feed her, bathe her, put her into clothes and get her back out of them again. She hadn't gotten to live a normal life until her mother had died and by then it was too late, her childhood had passed her by. She'd tried to go back to school, and that was where Richard had found her, feeling a very out-of-place freshman at college at the ripe age of twenty-five.

Arthur brought soup in, and it was delicious—less so the realization that to time presenting courses, Arthur and the mysterious Mrs. Dudley had to be watching her. Had they eaten yet? Were they waiting on her? She found herself eating more quickly as the meal progressed, racing an imaginary clock.

"Would you like a glass of wine?" Arthur asked, as he came out with asparagus and steak.

Normally, no, but after the day she'd had? "Please."

He smiled at her, and disappeared.

She was going to have to talk to Mrs. Dudley—she didn't eat much red meat, and Richard needed none of it. But it was a perfect medium rare, just how she liked, and the asparagus were yielding yet just a little crisp—and the wine, when Arthur reappeared, complimented the meal perfectly.

"Where did this come from?" she asked him, after he refilled her glass.

"From your very generous food budget, Ma'am. There's a wine cellar off of the kitchen. I think the former occupants left a few bottles behind."

She took another swig of wine. "And where do you and Mrs. Dudley live?"

"Hillsdale."

The nearest town, if it could be called that, one of those places seemingly comprised of antique stores that erupted at regular intervals once one drove out far enough into the country.

"And have you always been a…servant?" She hated using the word, but knew no other one to call him.

"Ever since I was a boy. I didn't start here, but I did end up here. I spent twenty years serving the Master in this house, before the next owners took over and released me. Your agent called me out of a long retirement."

"Oh, I'm so sorry," she apologized, and he looked appalled.

"Please, don't be. It was dreadfully boring, honestly."

She realized the wine had given her an excuse for familiarity—which clearly made Arthur uncomfortable. "And you go back to Hillsdale each night?"

"We do."

"I don't mean to keep you then. You should go. It's dark."

He measured her with his eyes, trying to tell if her kindness was a test or for show or genuine reality. "We will do the dishes tomorrow then. First thing."

"Any time you like. Honestly."

"And you know the code? And have the key?"

Daphne nodded. Richard had made sure she knew the code for their new home's security system, all the better to not have the security system call him with false alarms in the middle of the night in Abu Dhabi or wherever it was that the bank had sent him this week.

"All right then, Ma'am. We'll see ourselves out the back, it's where we've parked our car. We'll set the alarm as we go, so don't open any windows or outside doors."

"I won't."

Arthur paused then, seeming to come to a decision. "I don't want to scare you, Ma'am, but if you need help—call sooner than later. You're so far out from town, no one will hear you."

Daphne blinked. Some part of her had already known that, in the uncomfortable way that all women recognized—but she wasn't about to let on she was afraid. "I'll be fine," she said, with more bravery than she felt.

"Very good," Arthur said, and nodded. "What time would you like breakfast, Ma'am?"

She ought to say eight, but with as much wine as she'd had tonight? "Nine."

"Excellent. We'll see you then." He gave her another bow and then withdrew.

SHE HEARD the alarm chirp as Arthur set it on his way out. She was finally alone—it was a little frightening, but if she drank enough wine she wouldn't mind. She gathered her mother's china and followed Arthur's path back to the kitchen. It was more industrial than homey, meant to feed an army quickly if needbe. All the burners were off and things were clean—Mrs. Dudley was a neater cook than she'd ever been. Daphne put the dishes into the sink and turned the water on. She hadn't seen these dishes since her mother'd died. Everything had gone into boxes then, too.

Maybe she'd stay up all night to unpack. Maybe she'd push herself and get everything unpacked by next week, so that when Richard came home there'd be nothing to distract him, nothing for him to worry about, just her. She imagined him being pleased with how much she'd done, impressed with her choices, the angles at which she'd aligned the couches and chairs—and then imagined him taking her on one of them, as if to try out its feng shui. There were enough bedrooms here they could sleep in a new room every night of the week, a new position each time, until she finally got pregnant.

If she had a baby it would keep her company. This house wouldn't be half so lonely with a child in it—and half again as lonely after the second one. Until then, though—she scanned the countertop and saw the bottle of wine, its cork replaced—she could drink, a little. Someone ought to get to celebrate moving in.

Daphne took the stairs two at a time, until she found herself in her bedroom again. Her first night in her new home, alone. There were no curtains on the windows yet, the former occupants had taken them, so she stood in the window and looked out at the night. Cicadas hummed nearby, or were they crickets? She knew she ought to know. She dumped the last drops of tea onto the saucer Arthur had brought her earlier and poured a ration of wine into it, and then drank it so quickly she might as well have gulped straight from the bottle.

Richard couldn't make time for her now. What would change after a baby? Nothing. There'd be promises made and broken and she would cry, but things would always be the same. Richard was the kind of man who the world changed for—but he never changed for it.

She drank another tea-cup of wine and set the bottle down on her side table, uncorked, and pulled her clothing off roughly. She'd unpacked enough she wouldn't need to find out where the laundry was for at least a week, maybe more, but she hadn't found the box with her slips and nightgowns yet. So she got into bed naked, and pulled the sheets up to her neck.

Her dim bedside lamp light was filtered through the winebottle's green glass. She reached out and grabbed its neck, taking another deep swig, and then set it back. A woozy warmth suffused her now, emanating out from her belly, all of the wine caught up to her at last.

She turned off the light and just lay there, letting it carry her, as though she were a passenger on a ship on a tropical day.

For better or worse, this place was her new home. It creaked and groaned around her, settling in the night air, and while she wasn't scared, she felt incredibly alone. She hugged herself beneath the covers, arms under her own breasts, nipples rubbing against the sheets she'd pulled tight. Something—the alcohol, the abandonment, the spinning feeling she got as she let go—her hands pressed up under her breasts now, taking them one each, feeling her supple skin, their gentle weight.

She stroked one thumb over a nipple tentatively, to see if it would answer her, and it did, becoming pert and sending a line of electricity down between her legs. She did it again, as though she were strumming a guitar and felt the wave of pleasure pull and pluck, deep inside her hips, where she was restless and aching.

Even though she knew what would come next, she opened her mouth in surprise. Her other hand touched her thigh and started stroking, tracing fingers on herself like she liked Richard to tease her when he had the time, like she didn't know where her own hand would wind up, not even until it tickled between her closed thighs and they spread open to reveal her pussy like a book. Her lower hand waited then, as her higher one pulled at her nipple again, setting things aglow and then she pressed.

Her clit was like a button, and Richard the first lover to have found it, showing it to her again and again in one orgasmic night. Since then, she'd figured out how to push herself—how hard, how often, how fast. She brought up her hand and licked her fingertips for lesser friction— and soon she could dive her fingers into her own heat and use the wetness they found there. Daphne stroked and pulled and brought her feet up so that her hips could rise as her pussy tried to match her hand and found that all of her was getting warm. The temperature, a thermostat somewhere, left on—so much heat that she interrupted herself to throw the covers off, to writhe naked on the bed. The feeling of heat became more precise—like hands were pressing on her, her thighs, her stomach, her breasts, her belly. She knew they were only in her imagination because now she could see herself by the moonlight, the angles of her knees, her hips as they canted ever higher, as her ass rising as she felt the need to come —

"Yes," she pleaded with the night and anyone who could hear her. "Yes —" she panted, to herself, the word like a spell, pushing her closer to the brink, frantically stroking and pushing and pulling and—"Yes! Yes—yes—yes!"

She bucked in the bed as she came, sending it rocking, like her orgasm was fighting her. She gasped and she cried out again, finally freed—and she heard the wine bottle fall to the floor.

"Fuck!" Transcendence was instantly lost, and she fumbled for the light. Dribbles of wine were pouring out of the bottle onto the hardwood. She cursed and picked up the shirt she'd worn today and blotted at the wine before it could stain. There hadn't been that much left in the bottle, and the room was spinning now—she should have told Arthur to tell Mrs. Dudley ten at this rate.

Daphne stumbled into the bathroom with her shirt and clumsily tried to wash it, between forcing herself to drink giant gulps of water down. Then she crept, naked and abashed, back into bed.

CHAPTER 2

"Mrs. Vance?"

Daphne's eyes blinked open and saw only pillowcase.

"Mrs. Vance, are you all right?"

Daphne lurched up right in bed, and it felt like her head was slower than the rest of her, following two seconds behind. "I'm all right —" she said. The knob turned, and she realized she was naked. "Hang on!"

She was a mess, and she didn't want him to see. Daphne raced to the bathroom to pull on her robe and smooth her hair down.

"I'm sorry Arthur," she opened up the door just a crack, finding his implacable face standing a respectful distance outside. "I must've missed breakfast."

"It's no matter—but we were getting worried about you. Thought you might have gone exploring last night and gotten lost."

"Oh, no. Just a rough night is all." The wine bottle was still in her room. Would he find it when he went cleaning? They had to know it was missing, since it was no longer in the kitchen, and she had no idea where the recycling bin was, she couldn't even throw it away without their help.

"Can Mrs. Dudley make you lunch then?"

She wasn't hungry, but she needed to eat something real, to center herself. "Please. Something easy though—a sandwich—something light."

He nodded. "And then after that, you'll be unpacking all afternoon, I expect. Will you be requiring any help today? Or would you like me to continue in the library?"

"The library's fine. I'm not done in here. I was up late night, unpacking, and—" it was a better excuse than what had occurred. Besides, he wasn't going to come in here and pry, for all he knew everything in her bedroom was already unpacked.

"Very well, Ma'am. Lunch will be served shortly, thank you."

"No, thank you, Arthur. And Mrs. Dudley. Please thank her, too." Daphne said, and then retreated back into her bedroom.

WHAT'D HAPPENED LAST NIGHT? She'd drank too much, that was what. She needed to remember wherever she'd packed the ibuprofen. Daphne stumbled back into the bathroom and gulped handfuls of water from the sink, to solve her headache the old fashioned way. Then she brushed her teeth—another chore forgotten in last night's bender—and looked at herself. She didn't look nice enough for the bathroom, muchless the dining hall. Maybe there was a breakfast nook or someplace smaller that she could reclaim for eating. She pulled clothing out of her closet, pulled it on, and went downstairs.

A STEAK SANDWICH with artfully cut radishes and cucumbers and a side of freshly fried fries waited for her on the long table. She ate in lonely silence, listening to the quiet sound of her own chewing.

"Are you sated, Ma'am?" Arthur appeared in the doorway, three seconds after her last bite.

"Completely." She drained her glass of water. If she went upstairs, this might be the last human contact she had all day. He could bring her tea but she couldn't invite him into her bedroom, it wouldn't be right—and he might see the wine stain. She was suddenly reluctant to be without company, and glad he was present, even if he was paid. "Can you show me how the library's coming along?"

"I'd be delighted to."

ARTHUR LED her down a hall at the back of the dining room, to a massive windowed room on the other wing.

Looming over a fireplace set into the wall was a portrait almost as tall as she was. A handsome yet very stern man stared down, in riding breeches and knee high boots, holding a short crop in one hand and a snifter of brandy in the other.

Daphne walked in to stand beneath him and stared up, trying to read the painting's meaning, feeling penetrated by his eyes. His skin was pale but his eyes were dark, brooding, his cheekbones were painfully sharp, and his chin had a slight cleft. His full lips were pulled into a look of disdain, as though having his portrait painted was beneath him.

"As you can see, there's much work to be done," Arthur apologized, breaking her communion.

"Hmm?" She glanced around at the stacks of books lying all across the floor, and could see how Arthur was trying to come up with a system prior to putting them on the shelves that ran along the rest of the wall space. Richard had always fancied himself a reader, but the books they had would only occupy a fraction of the space of the man had once ruled here. Perhaps that was why he looked so displeased— he was angry over the loss of his own books.

"It's going to be another day or two," Arthur went on.

"That's fine. Richard won't be home for six more days."

Instead of looking out the window, or at the spines of books that she'd all seen before, the portrait mesmerized her. His eyes seemed to blaze with barely restrained passion—or disgust.

"Who is that?" she finally asked, as Arthur began to putter.

He looked up. "The Master, in his prime."

"That's who lived here?"

"Lived and died here. He was born just down the hall, and died peacefully at night in his own bed."

"He…died here? Not in a hospital or anything?"

Arthur's lips drew into a thin line. "The Master always was one to face life on his own terms. Death was no exception."

It was handsome as art for art's sake—portraits that size were expensive, and the gilded frame alone had to be worth a few thousand dollars. "Why did they leave it behind?"

Arthur briefly shrugged. "I don't know. The branch of the family that was left in the will—I hate to speak ill of anyone, but they seemed a little odd. They were very adamant about what they would take, and what would be left behind, like the statues and the pieces of furniture. And then the next family kept things as they were when they arrived, and chose not to take them when they left either."

"Did you work for them?" she asked him, while still staring up.

"Oh no, only for him. I was retired for fifteen years, until your agent called me back, but because the interim family left so much behind, the place still feels much the same. Would you like an official tour?"

She finally tore her eyes away from the painting. "I'd love one."

"After you then, Ma'am," Arthur said, indicating the direction she should go. It wasn't until halfway down the next hall she shook the feeling that the painting was watching her back.

ARTHUR SHOWED her all of the rooms on the first floor, even the kitchen, although Mrs. Dudley was suspiciously absent. Maybe she was a ghost and Arthur was, in addition to his other skills, an excellent cook.

Many of the rooms were airy and light, especially now at noon. They all needed a good airing out, and different furniture—between the two families, such strange things were left behind, huge carved couches, desks, a crib, some rooms empty, one full of the strange statues, clustered together as though huddled for warmth. Maybe the

Master's family had only been able to afford one moving truck and had started flipping quarters at the end to see what would fit.

The most important thing though was that she could imagine a child running from room to room, and her running after them, both of them laughing along the way. The epic games of hide-and-seek she could have in this house, once her child—no, *children*—were old enough—in the bright light of day. Maybe moving here would be worth it after all.

When their tour was done, she felt bad for taking Arthur away from his work, and she wanted to finish unpacking the bedroom, so she begged off.

"What time dinner, Ma'am?" Arthur called after her.

"Seven. And—the steak was excellent, but can tonight be chicken?"

"Of course, Ma'am."

She smiled and waved to him like he was a friend, and trotted back up the stairs.

DAPHNE FOUND her own room as light and airy as those downstairs, a welcome change after her overheated claustrophobia the prior night. She whirled in a circle, making her skirt lift, before falling onto her own bed like a swooning girl.

She could almost see a future for her here. It would be hard work, but she'd enjoy it, and with Richard by her side—she smiled and came up onto her elbows to survey the unpacking she'd already done, and noticed that her closet door was open—and now she could see herself, frowning in the mirror on the inside of the door.

She got out of bed slowly and took deliberate steps across the room. She swung it on its hinges—it didn't seem light. And when she closed it again she felt it latch, like she was almost positive it had been this morning, earlier.

Why would anyone snoop now? When there was so much more unpacking to do? And why a closet? It wasn't like she had anything valuable in there, she didn't own any furs—and before they'd moved,

Richard'd scooped up all of her jewelry and put it in a safe deposit box.

It couldn't have been Arthur, he'd been with her the whole time. Which left Mrs. Dudley, and her knees that weren't so bad she couldn't snoop.

"My second day here, and already I have to fire someone." She sat back down on the bed, and the feeling of betrayal and invasion didn't lessen.

SEVEN FOUND HER DOWNSTAIRS, wondering what to do. Dinner was an entire roast chicken, far too much meat for one person—a chicken sandwich was mostly likely on the lunch menu for tomorrow.

Assuming Mrs. Dudley was still here, then.

"How was dinner, Ma'am?" Arthur asked, after she finished a small bowl of pudding.

"It was excellent, again."

How far away was the nearest town? Who would she find to replace Mrs. Dudley, and how? She hadn't unpacked their computer, muchless installed internet yet, and cell phone service this far into the country side was a joke. So the only way she could replace Mrs. Dudley would be to use the old fashioned landline—assuming that there was a phone book written this century hidden somewhere inside the house.

"I'm glad to hear it, Ma'am," Arthur said, taking her bowl away with a bow. "Mrs. Dudley says to please not do the dishes again. That is her job, after all. A servant does like to feel that they're gainfully employed."

"Well tell her to stay out of my closet then," Daphne said, flustered.

"Ma'am?" Arthur said, eyebrows high in surprise.

If Mrs. Dudley was at all like Arthur—and his familiarity and trust in her implied she was—then—Daphne shook her head at herself. It could have been a thousand other things. This house was old, it'd settled over time, and maybe she hadn't closed the door as strongly as she thought she had this morning, while still in the grip of her hangover.

"I'm sorry Arthur," she apologized, instantly deflating.

"Of course, Ma'am. But there's nothing to apologize for." He looked at her like a baffled dog. "What time would you like breakfast, Ma'am?"

There'd been no wine involved in dinner tonight—she wanted to stay well away from it for now. "Let's say eight."

"Very good, Ma'am. When we leave, we'll set the alarm and lock the doors."

Daphne nodded, stood, and pushed in her chair. Firing Mrs. Dudley would have to wait for another day, if ever.

ALONE IN THE HOUSE, she retreated to her bedroom again. This afternoon's efforts had seen it almost half done—Richard's closet was organized now in a way that she knew he'd find pleasing upon his return. Her own was nearing completion and their antique dresser was now full of mated socks and folded underwear.

She'd be pleased with her progress, except for the stain the wine had left on the floor. It'd set by the time she'd gotten up this morning and in her drunkenness she hadn't done a thorough job of cleaning it last night. The old wood had drunk the pinot up and now there was a smeared stain, like a lazy trail of blood. Maybe she should just pull the bed over three feet to the left, and put a duster on it. Then no one would ever have to know.

No matter. She wouldn't be drinking in here again—bedroom drinking was how people became alcoholics, she was sure.

Daphne took off her clothing, brushed her teeth, and pulled on a robe and lay down, completely awake. She wished she had a TV to watch mindlessly—she knew there was one somewhere in the boxes downstairs, but which one and where it ought to go after she found it she was unsure of. But it wasn't fair that she had to pass all of her time unpacking—and then she remembered the library.

. . .

DAPHNE SHUFFLED across the house in bare feet, turning lights on along the way, realizing how exposed and bright the house would look if there were anyone peeking in from outside. It was a disturbing thought, how open it was, probably the only light for miles around, but she was too scared to turn the lights back off. Curtains would definitely be her next priority.

But the library felt safe once she reached it. The books smelled of Richard, of stability and age. And the portrait of the Master looking down—while she found him pleasantly stern, she thought anyone else would find him threatening.

She walked among the hip-high stacks, bending over to scan familiar titles, looking for something new or something very, very old and comfortable to read. She found two books that she knew she enjoyed, carefully pulled them out, and held them up.

"Which one do you think I should pick?" she asked the man in the painting on a whim. "Lady Chatterley's Lover? Or Rebecca?" She waited half-a-second, smirking up at him. "What's the matter? Cat got your tongue?"

This brief moment of control and whimsy realigned her. Made her feel like she was mistress of the house again, as unfamiliar as it was. She walked out of the library and back to her room, her robe trailing her like a train.

DAPHNE CRAWLED into bed and began reading about Lady Chatterly's Lover. It wasn't long before the book dropped forward on her chest and she began to dream.

In it, she rode endlessly riding toward a horizon, rocking back and forth on a horse's broad back. Heat built where her legs split and met the saddle, bouncing with every move the horse made, translating the beginnings of pleasure into her, if she could just let herself go. In her dream the horse had no reins and she wound her hands into its mane to hold on as the saddle disappeared and left her grinding against its sweating black back, every motion it made beneath her safe and strong. It raced toward a horizon that—in the manner of dreams—it would never reach, and she began to moan.

The horse's back got bigger, spread her legs more widely and the friction between it and her became more intense. She knew she should be ashamed of even thinking such thoughts, but she knew it was a dream, and in her dream she wanted to let go—

A soft click from the outside world intruded and she startled awake. The sensation of riding didn't end though—because she could clearly feel the outline of hot hands spreading open her thighs.

She screamed, snapping her legs together, sitting straight up. The book fell from her chest to the ground.

CHAPTER 3

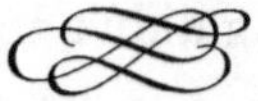

"Who's there?" She looked around the empty room—and saw where her closet door was open, just a crack.

"I mean it—" she fumbled in her nightstand drawer for the remote that controlled the alarm. She didn't care where in the world Richard was now, they could very well wake him, even if it was all in her head—

But the light had been on when she woke up—there was no way there could be anyone else in the room with her now. She would have seen them, they'd had no time to hide. She squirmed in bed, an uncomfortable heat still lingering between her thighs. She stood, and walked over to the closet, looking inside of it, and finding only herself in the mirror. And then she checked out Richard's closet, and the bathroom just in case.

The feeling of danger faded, replaced by curiosity. "I'm not the crazy one, am I?" she asked, well aware that just asking it made it much more likely that she was.

She slid herself back up to the head of the bed, and picked up her book. Lady Chatterley's Lover had all sorts of provocative horseriding scenes, and her dream had clearly come from that, it was a normal thing. But the sound of her closet door falling open—it was one more thing she needed to fix, and good thing she hadn't fired Mrs. Dudley earlier, such a good thing—had startled her and in her half-asleep state she'd assumed the worst.

Right?

She set Lady Chatterley's Lover down and picked up Rebecca instead. And when she felt tired she set the book aside but left the light on.

DAPHNE MET Arthur for breakfast downstairs at eight on the dot. He seemed pleased to see her and for Mrs. Dudley's culinary talents not to go to waste.

"And what are your plans today, Ma'am?" Arthur asked, after she had eaten a polite amount of everything and the table needed to be cleaned.

Daphne bit her lip. The bedroom was nearly finished, she couldn't just hide in there anymore. "I'm going to give myself a tour of the second floor, and see where I should turn my attentions next."

"Very well, Ma'am. I hope to finish the library today, if I do I will find you and ask for instruction."

"Thank you Arthur," she said, pushing her chair back from the table. "And thank Mrs. Dudley too, that was lovely."

He bowed politely, and she left.

DAPHNE TOOK her time walking up the stairs. She wasn't tired, though she ought to be, since she'd left the light on all night. Instead, she felt excited—invigorated, even—at the chance to see the rest of the house, in the bright light of day.

The upstairs was organized into two massive wings, accessible only from the wide-winged stairs in the hallway out front. She felt like a detective, trying to piece together what each room had been. Four old divots in the hardwood, as if from a desk? Then perhaps it'd been a study. An abandoned piano in one room—a conservatory? She plinked out a few tentative notes and listened to them echo before moving on. Many of the rooms had massive beds, but little other furniture—and halfway through she realized she'd started thinking of the people who'd come through after the Master had died as locusts, stealing away the home's rightful furnishings, like the curtains and the portraits from the dining room's walls. No wonder the statues seemed so upset—they'd had to watch everything else around them get taken away.

She tried all the faucets in the bathrooms—they were done in garish shades of lime green and pink, and they'd all need remodeling too, if she could get contractors out this far—and flushed all the toilets, making sure they worked. As she walked from room to room, inspecting doors and closets, looking out each window's view, she began to feel a sense of ownership. She may have been abandoned here, but this place was hers, already so much more than it was Richard's, even if the only reason they could afford it was because of his deep pocketbook.

She trotted down the stairs again, across the cold tile of the entryway, and up to the other wing's second floor.

This side was all bedrooms, one after another, politely divided by more garish bathrooms. They were all empty, except for a few more statues, and one enormous room holding a massive four poster bed.

Its mattresses were as high as her hips. It had enormous clawed feet and the posters were only inches below the ceiling in height. She walked across the room to it slowly because it looked like a living thing, like it might come alive and attack her. There were no sheets on it, nothing to hide the elaborate carving that held the mattresses in on all four sides, roughly hewn symbols of a bygone time, roaring lions, sleeping dragons, and a brace of running wolves taking down a bucking unicorn. Someone must have commissioned it, because she was familiar with antiques in a general sense, and she had never seen its like.

Daphne slowed as she reached its end. A feeling of warmth overcame her—a flush of embarrassment, she thought, because it was impossible to stand at the bottom of this kind of bed without imagining being bent over it, ass in the air, being taken from behind. The longer she thought on the image the more turned on she was, and her pussy began a low familiar ache. Richard was gone so often—and still gone, now. She swallowed, and remnants of last night's half-forgotten dream returned, how close she'd been to coming then, before her fear denied her.

Heat gathered inside her hips. She shouldn't stay here, she should run back to her own bedroom and finish herself off, be able to stroke her own clit and push welcome fingers inside—when she felt the distinct outline of a hot hand press against her leg and move up.

Daphne yelped as if caught, and whirled around. No one was there. But she'd felt it, it'd burned her almost, it felt as hot as her pussy was—and maybe just as hungry.

But she *was* alone. She stood there panting, half in fear, half in need, trying to convince herself that what she'd felt had been real and not sure at all that that was a good idea.

If it hadn't been daylight, if birds hadn't been singing outside, and if Arthur and Mrs. Dudley hadn't been puttering in the library and kitchen downstairs respectively, she might not have continued—but because it was, and they were, she took a crazy chance.

"I know you're there. You can come out, if you want."

A hot hand squeezed her own. She gasped and stepped aside.

"I'm—not insane, am I? Are you…real?"

Whatever or whoever it was decided not to honor that.

"Who are you?"

The hand squeezed her own again, and she had the sensation of someone taller than she was standing very close. She could feel the heat radiating off of their unseen body all along her own.

"Did you used to live here?"

The sensation of nearness did not decrease.

"Did you live in this room?" she guessed. "In this house?" she clarified. In response, she felt one warm finger trail down her arm. She shuddered at the contact, not in fear, but in pleasure—and was instantly ashamed and horrified.

"I have to—" she stepped aside, away from the heat, and ran, both frightened and turned on. She slammed the door shut behind her, hoping to hide from whatever it was in the room with her and her feelings.

SHE RACED down the stairs and into the library, where the Master's portrait looked down disdainfully at the progress Arthur had made.

"Arthur—" she began, breathless.

"Ma'am?" He startled straight at the sight of her. "Do you need tea? Lunch will be—"

"No, no—um," Now that she was here with him, she wasn't sure what to ask without feeling foolish. "Can you tell me some of this house's history?"

He blinked. "I was only here for the last twenty years of the Master's life, and other than his interest in carving furniture, there's not much to tell."

"Have you…ever seen a ghost here?"

He seemed to consider this. "A house this old has history, no doubt. And history, almost by default, includes ghosts. But no, I've never seen one."

Daphne chewed the inside of her lip. "Never?"

"Never," he said, shaking his head solemnly. "It is spooky here sometimes though. So much open space, so little life. Perhaps you should buy some houseplants? Orchids would go nicely with your décor. Or take in a cat or dog. I can arrange that in town, if you'd wish."

She shook her head quickly. The thought of a cat staring off into space watching something she couldn't see didn't appeal to her much.

"Perhaps can I interest you in some tea?"

"I'd like that."

She sagged into the sitting couch as Arthur left the room. He was

right about one thing—there was history here. And the family that'd
lived here after the Master had died had done little to erase it.

Daphne looked down at her arms. She'd felt it, hadn't she? It had
touched her—it had been real.

But who was it?

A lazy breeze made the shadows of the trees outside wave across
the ground. She watched them for a time, and when she looked up she
saw the Master staring down.

DAPHNE FINISHED UNPACKING the bedroom that day and didn't go
exploring again. Dinner was a quiet affair, she ate because she needed
to eat, nothing more.

"Are you sure you're well?" Arthur'd asked solicitously at the end
of the evening.

"I am." She wasn't, not at all. But she'd been thinking about it, all
afternoon.

She didn't want to tell Arthur about it and sound crazy. The ghost,
if ghost it was, hadn't tried to harm her. There'd been no parlor tricks,
no flies beating against the windows, or blood dripping from the
ceiling—nothing frightening, just a presence nearby. If this had been
her home for eighty years, wouldn't she want to vet the new owners
too? And she didn't want to go in with guns blazing, hiring a priest, as
if their mumbo-jumbo-malarkey would even work. No, there had to
be a way to come to an amicable agreement—an understanding—
between the two of them, to live here in peace.

The house was certainly big enough.

She heard the alarm chirp on and calmly walked upstairs. If the
ghost had wanted her dead, he'd already had two nights to do her in.
And he hadn't tried to scare her yet—he'd just wanted to make his
presence known.

DAPHNE CLOSED the bedroom door behind herself and swallowed
before speaking. "You're still here, right?"

Nothing. No heat, no sensation of anyone else in the room. She didn't know if she should be angry or relived.

"Hello?" she tried again. Where else would a ghost have to be? She smirked, imagining him going off to a ghostly dental appointment—when the feeling of being watched began, wiping the smirk off of her face.

"You're here."

Nothing touched her. No heat. Just that skin prickling feeling that was as intense as being turned on.

"I don't think I'm afraid of you. I mean I am—but—I shouldn't be, right?"

A warm hand took hers and pulled her to her bedside, as though she and the ghost were girlfriends about to have a difficult conversation. She sat down, ankles crossed, her skirt pulling just above her knee.

"We live here now. But there's no reason for you to go anywhere. This house is definitely big enough for the two of us. Three of us, if you count Richard—although I realize you haven't seen him yet."

The hand that'd been around her own disappeared—and reappeared, on her knee, like a familiar lover's.

"He's very nice. You would like him if you met him. I know you would," she said, talking faster as the hand moved fractionally up her thigh. "I mean, we're married, and, he's only gone because he has to be. He's in the banking business and—" The sensation of heat crept higher along her bare skin and underneath the front edge of her skirt. Daphne saw the fabric ripple, allowing him access beneath, the edge of a hand, an arm, as she felt fingers stroke the inside of her thigh.

"And I know he loves me—he must, mustn't he? He bought me this whole house—" she went on, as the heat rose. She knew she should be running away, be hiding in a closet, be setting off the alarm. But every motion the hand made created a warm flutter inside her, echoing its motion, and she found herself experiencing it as though she were in a movie, waiting to see just how far it would go, how far she would let it go, if she would—could—even stop it.

She was holding her breath now, and the hand stilled, grabbing hold of her inner thigh, fingers, thumb, and palm all hot, mere inches below what her underwear hid. She could feel her pussy ache, empty for so long, wet and scared and excited now.

"You won't hurt me, will you?" she whispered to a seemingly empty room.

There was no reply.

✕

CHAPTER 4

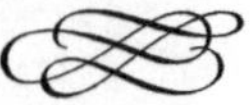

Another hand joined the first one, pushing her knees apart. Daphne inhaled to scream, then realized the futility of it, as they were completely alone. She squirmed, but his hands held her in place, opening her thighs wide on the edge of the bed, her skirt edging ever higher.

She gasped—she'd been a fool to invite this, to think she could handle this alone when—she felt the pressure of a tongue, as hot as the rest of him, lapping at her clit through her underwear.

The sound she was about to make, shouting stop, no, go away, changed to panting disbelief as she stared down. There was nothing to see, she could only feel what was going on, but it was…incredible. She moaned without thinking and the tongue below sped up. Even through her underwear, the friction was intense.

She bent over, looking down, imagining the man there looking up. "How? Why?"

He didn't stop to answer her. His tongue just kept pressing, stroking, circling and pushing at her clit through the thin piece of fabric. Her hips began to rise and her legs spread of their own accord to offer more of herself to him. But if she were going to come—she needed more.

If she was going to do this, then *let it be done right.*

She reached down. She didn't want to reach through him, that would be rude at best, at worst it would banish him, so she carefully slid her hand down and—nervous again—pulled the crotch of her underwear aside, exposing herself to him.

He paused, and for a moment she thought he'd disappeared, that she'd scared him off—and then his tongue regained her and she could feel the heat of him directly on her clit, now with lips too, him kissing her there, hard, and then feel him slide his tongue between her labia to press in-in-in.

She moaned long and low. She rocked back on the bed, falling onto it, giving herself over to his mouth. She never felt the pressure or strength of a finger, only his tongue, lips, and the outline of a chin, all hot, licking and sucking, as though they might never get to taste a woman again.

Her hips rose even higher as she went on her tip-toes and her free hand wound in the sheet beside her ass. She could feel her orgasm building, stoking like a volcano, and everything he was doing was going to make her explode—his chin pushing in, his lips sucking hard and his hot tongue dancing across her clit, writing in letters of flame.

She shuddered, hips bobbing, and she screamed as she came. His mouth followed her, sucking her last juices out as her orgasm flowed through her, leaving her moaning on the bed.

Time stopped, or felt like it did. Daphne let go of the sheets slowly, feeling as wrung out as she had made them.

"Ghost?" she tried out the unfamiliar term. Was ghost really what you called someone who'd just given you what you'd wanted so thoroughly?

There was no response. No feeling of heat, no sensation of otherness. The space between her legs was cooling now without his presence there.

Daphne sat up, supporting herself on both arms and looked down. Her skirt was as disheveled as she was. Was that—had that—been real? How could it have been? But—it was. She'd felt it. She'd felt *him.*

She pulled her legs up on the bed with her and curled up. The philosophical questions she could ask herself took second place to the fact that she was completely satisfied now, in a way she hadn't been since Richard'd left, and without undressing she slept.

DAPHNE WOKE at six AM the next morning. All that'd come before felt like a dream—but she was still in this house, and still in her clothes. And the memory of last night rushed back—her inviting the ghost in, and then letting him have his way with her—she shook her head. It hadn't felt like cheating at the time, and there was no proof it'd even happened, yet it left a bitter residue.

She stumbled through the empty house to the landline phone downstairs and dialed Richard's cell. She'd tell him what'd happened and he wouldn't believe her, he'd tell her she'd been dreaming, and that would be that. Her conscience wouldn't be completely clean, but it would be freshly laundered.

She picked up the old fashioned phone and dialed and sank down to sit with her back against the wall, waiting for her long distance call to go through.

"Hello?" answered a woman on the far end of the line.

"Hello?" Daphne said, much more sharply. "Who is this?"

A moment of hesitation, and then, "This is Richard's secretary."

After last night, Daphne was sure of very little in this world—other than the fact that that woman was not her husband's secretary.

"Who is this?" the other woman asked her.

"This is Richard's wife. Put him on the phone. Immediately."

There was a pause and she heard voices in the background, before Richard picked up. "Pet—how are you? What time is it there? Is everything okay?"

Daphne licked her lips in thought. "Everything's fine. I just wanted to hear your voice was all. What time is it there? Where is there?"

"Tokyo. It's 3 PM. You managed to catch me in between meetings."

"You and your secretary," she said, clinically.

"The banks here always provide you with clerical staff, yes. Never know when you're going to need to write an urgent memo."

"Of course." *Sound reasonable, Daphne. Don't let anything on.*

"So—" She could hear the hesitance in Richard's voice, not wanting to own up to being caught if he didn't have to. "Everything is fine?"

She swallowed. "Yes. I just thought you should know how much I love our new house."

"I'm so glad. I can't wait to see what you've done to the bedroom," he said in a voice that sounded like he thought he was off the hook.

He was—but only for now. "I can't wait to show you. When are you coming home?"

"Business is taking longer than usual—I'm afraid I won't be home from a week from today."

Daphne frowned. Gone for longer, and with that other woman…. "But you'll be home then?" she asked, her voice small.

"Most certainly."

"Good. I can't wait to see you."

"Me either, pet. Love you."

"Love you too," she said, and heard him hang up.

DAPHNE HUNG up the phone more slowly on her end. It was the first name that did it. She could have convinced herself otherwise, if the woman hadn't used his first name. Secretaries—especially assigned ones—were not that familiar.

How long had it been going on? Did he have a woman in every port? Or was it just this one time? How would she know? How could she ever, ever, trust him again?

Daphne wandered through the downstairs halls, herself like a ghost, crying bitter tears, until she wound up in the library. Dawn was peeking over the edge of the world and the books Arthur had already put up were basking in a warm light.

She stood in front of the portrait of the Master, looking up into his piercing eyes.

"I—I don't want to be alone." She whispered the words, to herself first, and to him second.

Then she felt him in the room, like a rush of warm rain, and she found herself pushed bodily against the nearest shelf, his heat all over the front of her body, him kissing the tears off of her face and his hands racing down her sides. She gasped at the onslaught, fighting, not-fighting, relenting, basking in the heat of his raw desire.

And then the alarm chirped as Arthur and Mrs. Dudley arrived, and the ghost instantly departed. Daphne almost fell to the ground, cold without his warmth—and then she gathered herself, running upstairs up to her bedroom to hide.

SHE DIDN'T FEEL his presence at all that day. It was like she was listening for a sound once familiar but now forgotten, a half-remembered song. She unpacked the den and half of the office, turning around any time she thought she might have heard something, always finding nothing there.

But she knew he wasn't gone—and she had no doubt that he was watching her. Not after this morning, when he'd been beside her in an instant. He was just waiting, biding his time, until he could have her again, alone.

He wanted her. *He* was waiting for her. Instead of thinking about Richard off with that other woman—and how many other women there might be—Daphne chose to concentrate on *him* instead.

Everything she did she did as though she might be watched. When she bent over to put low objects away, she made sure to keep her ass up high. And when she reached for things, she did so with her breasts up, all the better to show them off to apparently thin air. The game made her feel alive, and she found to her surprise that that that was even more important than being distracted from Richard's betrayal.

She ate dinner that night with impeccable manners, pretending that she had a dinner guest at the opposite end of the table. Once, when Arthur wasn't looking, she raised her wine glass in a subtle toast to where she thought he sat. And afterwards, when she heard the alarm chirp and knew they'd locked the door, she rose up and walked slowly, majestically, out to the entry hall and up to the stairs, her clit thumping with every step.

CHAPTER 5

When she reached the bedroom, she closed the door behind herself so that they would feel alone.

"Are you here?"

She knew he was, she knew that she could feel him, everywhere and nowhere both at once.

"Don't taunt me," she pleaded.

Hot hands cupped her ass, and she felt a wall of heat behind her. She moaned and leaned back, felt the pressure of his presence and then—she tumbled to the ground, skirt and ankles in the air. The sensation of heat evaporated.

She laughed at her own foolishness from the ground. "It's not you. It's me. I'm sorry."

She stood up, shaking her head at herself, walking over to the bed to sit down.

Her closet door opened then, fully, showing her the mirror hidden inside. She was sitting in the exact right place for it, she could see all of herself in its length.

She didn't know what to do next. Stretch her hands out to him, as if asking him to join her on the bed? That seemed too forward, and yet—she took the hem of her skirt between her hands and pulled it up, and then quickly pulled her underwear down and kicked it off. He had to know what she wanted—but would he be willing to give it to her again?

She felt a spot of heat on the inside of her left ankle. She thought it was a hand at first, then decided it was a kiss, as it lifted higher, drawing a line up the inside of her calf and then her thigh. She got an idea and let the fabric of her skirt float down, so that she could see the outline of his head as he rose up between her legs again. Daphne watched, distracted from his kisses, trying to envision the man underneath, and he reached up to push the fabric back.

"You're no fun," she said with a tease.

He pinched her inner thigh in complaint. She yelped, but then he kissed the spot he'd hurt—and he was a ghost besides, she'd fallen through him earlier, he couldn't really hurt her, right?

Both his hands pushed her thighs open for his tongue. She purred as he started sucking at her again, skirt forgotten—and then she felt one of the hands on her thighs slide up and hot fingers creep up to the entrance of her pussy.

"I'm—" she protested, and he stopped. What? She wasn't a virgin. And Richard was off with some 'secretary' halfway across the world. "Do it," she breathed, and fingers pushed in.

She moaned as lonely nerves lit up. His hot fingers probed into her as his mouth sucked on her clit and every time she looked up she saw herself in the mirror, eyes heavy, eager legs spread wide. It embarrassed her to see herself like this, but she found she couldn't look away—and when his other hand snaked up underneath her shirt and bra to cup her breast and pinch her nipple, she found she couldn't lean back even if she wanted to.

There was no need for conversation since he couldn't talk, and since she couldn't see his face, there was no need to be ashamed. Everything his hands or tongue did said he wanted her, he wanted to service her, he wanted her to be happy. She wasn't twelfth or twentieth on his list, behind a job and a mysterious secretary. He hadn't bought her a house to buy off his guilt. No—his thumb rolled over her nipple just like his tongue covered her clit and his fingers inside of her moved faster, stretching against the walls of her pussy in increasingly delicious ways. She saw herself in the mirror, panting, crouched over him on the edge of the bed, like some sort of needy beast, wanting more—

And that was why he'd opened the door with the mirror, she realized. Because while she couldn't lean back into him—he wanted her to know that he could do *this* to her—make her feel like this, take her from being the mistress of the house to a beggar in a day.

Forced to watch herself being turned on, being used—she was flooded with shame which, oddly, made everything hotter. Her pussy began to quiver around his fingers and his mouth redoubled its efforts on her clit and a moan began to build in the back of her throat. She saw herself tilt her head back to scream it out—she shouted and she writhed, hips bucking against the bed and the heat of his hands, forced to watch herself ride him, thrashing like a mermaid pulled onto a rocky shore.

Moments later, the sensation of his presence stopped, and the heat of her body was hers alone. Daphne staggered to standing and closed the closet door.

After a moment's thought she took off all her clothing with purposeful nonchalance and slid into bed.

SHE STAYED up as long as she could without saying a word.

Daphne didn't want to ask. She didn't want to have to. She'd spent so many nights asking Richard that—her face twisted into her pillow and she sighed. Was it any wonder she wasn't pregnant yet when she had to beg him to fuck her? Was it any wonder that he wasn't interested, when he was getting serviced around the globe?

When she'd abandoned hope of more, sleep came to her slowly, unfurling like a night-blooming flower—which was why she didn't believe it when it began, because it could have been a dream.

Daphne felt a weight in the bed behind her, moving in, and then a wall of heat against her exposed back, spooning her as she lay on her side.

He was here for her. He still wanted her—and from the tension and pressure and heat folded up against the cleft of her ass, she knew he wanted more of her than he had had so far.

A hot arm draped over her and reached for her breast. He thrust slowly behind her, rubbing himself against her, letting her know he was there and what he sought out….

And, half-asleep, half-awake, she knew she was going to give it to him. It'd been so long since Richard had turned to her like this, had needed her as badly as she felt like she needed him. She lifted her upper leg up and felt him move down her body until his hot cock was aligned and then slowly, slowly, he thrust up.

The head of his cock pushed into her, hot and hard. She wasn't ready for him, but she didn't want to be. She whined, an animal sound, lifting her leg higher as he pushed more in, somehow sensing that she needed this strange roughness to feel right. And the sudden sweetness of his cock shoving deep inside her, when they were matched, mated, like a key to a lock—relief flooded her as wetness did and he started to stroke.

She threw her head back into his chest and felt it solidly there. She was pinned on him now, and even though she knew she could get free, she didn't want to break the illusion of that. His hips rocked against hers and she moved in time, feeling his heat slide in and out, the head of him almost emerging, teasing the entrance of her pussy, before being rammed back inside.

She was content to be taken, pleased to be used—but a hand dove over her hips and went between her thighs and started to rub. She moved to push it away, she didn't deserve to pleased again so soon— but then thought better of it in time and instead held his hand steady with her own, forcing him to rub at her clit the way her pussy was rubbing his cock.

If he'd been a man really in bed with her—if he'd been Richard—he already would have come by now.

But by virtue of who and what he was—the only name she had to give him, Master, apt—she knew she was going to get to come again, first.

She pressed his hand tighter to her clit, felt his other hand grab roughly at her breast, felt the friction between them speed up as he rode her so thoroughly, held tight and being helplessly fucked—she screamed for the second time that night, with the abandon of those who know that no one else will hear, until her throat was hoarse. She spasmed on the bed and his cock kept riding her until the very end when it, still stiff, pulled out.

Daphne turned back in bed as the sensation of heat faded. "Don't go—" she said, but she knew she was alone.

CHAPTER 6

*D*aphne woke up bleary eyed but clear headed the next morning. She showered, blow dried her hair, and put on a cute outfit involving a short skirt, then went down for breakfast.

Arthur served her diligently. Did he know that she'd cheated on Richard? With a ghost, no less? She got a sly smile at the absurdity of it all, and the space between her legs became warm at the memory.

She was planning her escape back up to the bedroom at the end of the meal when Arthur announced, "Ma'am, the gardeners have arrived. Would you like to go and meet them, and make your needs known?"

She set her spoon down, feeling a guilty rush. "My needs?"

"In the garden. There's beds outside, now fallow, for herbs and vegetables—not to mention all the topiary and trees."

"Oh, yes, of course."

"I thought you might enjoy getting out of the house some today, too," Arthur said with a smile. "I'll let them know you're on your way."

"Thank you."

. . .

SHE FELT a little over dressed to be seeing gardeners. Still, if they were same as Arthur, from the home's original number, she might be meeting the elderly.

She followed Arthur out the back door and around the first line of shrubs, lawnmowers droning in the background. "Mr. Sanderson, may I present Mrs. Vance," Arthur said, with a bow, before dismissing himself.

And while she'd dressed this morning to tease the ghost in particular, at seeing Mr. Sanderson, she was very glad she had.

He was tan, broad shouldered, and very muscular, with a wide chin. She would have never imagined she'd find a man like him in the middle of nowhere like here.

"Please, call me Daphne."

"I'm Luke," he said, offering his hand out. She took it, and it was strong and warm.

"So—you're the gardener?" she said, unsure where to start.

"No, I'm the landscape professional," he corrected her. Daphne looked down, feeling chastised, until she heard him laugh and looked up to see his grin. "Really, I'm the 'you're-paying-me-enough-to-be-whatever-you-want.'"

She snorted softly and hoped she stopped herself from smirking in time.

"Let me show you around," he said, and started to walk. She trotted to catch up.

"We come out here a lot, depending on the season—it's a grand estate, there's a lot to do to keep it as is. If you want changes though, all you have to do is tell me."

"I don't know what I want yet, honestly. I've been so busy inside the house I haven't had a chance to look around."

"That what I'd thought. But it's planting season—the family that was here before you had a garden out back that they chose to tend on their own. It's gone a little wild now, but if you have a green thumb you can touch it up. Or we can do it for you."

"I'm sure you all have quite enough to do with all the lawn and the trees."

His smile was warm. "We can always do more, if you just let us know."

He said it like it was an invitation. Daphne swallowed, feeling as if a lead weight had dropped into her hips, and all the things she could ask him for help with leapt to mind. She shook her head—she would have never considered anything with anyone else ever before—had one night with the ghost changed her mind?

"Were you thinking of bringing horses in?" he asked, as she wrestled with her imagination.

"No, why?"

"I thought that might have been why you bought the place. There's a pasture out back. If you were I was going to reseed it for them."

She'd ridden before, back before her mother's illness and Richard. "I might—is there a stable?"

"Sure—just behind that copse of trees." He pointed along the path they walked. "It needs some maintenance—it's just as old as the house is, and the prior owners let it go at the end. My men can do that too, if you want—just give me about six weeks notice, before you go bringing in a horse."

"I will."

They reached a clearing where the din of the lawnmowers lessened, halfway to the stable. She was walking just to walk now, and he seemed content to walk with her.

"Do you know any of the history of this place?"

"Only what I've heard in town—and what the old owners told me. I know it's old, and people in town say it's haunted."

"By who?"

He shrugged broad shoulders. "Russians? When I was little, people would tell stories about the place. But honestly, you're so far back from the road, most people in town don't remember it at all."

"Russians? Really?"

"The old owners didn't think that was right, either."

"Why'd they leave?"

He made a pained face, as if holding truth back from her cost him. "They were happy enough at first—had a lot of friends in from out of town, dinner parties. But then," he started slowing down, as if weighing the former occupant's right to privacy. "Well, things changed after their daughter died."

"Oh no—how?"

He winced. "Horse riding accident. I—I shouldn't have brought it up—"

"No, I used to ride, I know how dangerous it can be."

Her admission relieved him somewhat. "She had this big black warmblood. Gorgeous beast, but an animal nonetheless."

"What happened to it afterward?"

"They sold it, I'm sure. And then the house was never the same after that. They didn't want to sell here—too many good memories, I suppose—but they moved out soon after. Kept us on this whole time. I don't know if they were hoping they could come back someday, or if they just realized the home would never sell if the grounds got too wild."

They were almost to the stable's door. It was a looming barn-roofed structure, two stories tall, and the angle of the morning light shadowed its open door, keeping the inside cool and dark. She wanted to investigate, but knew on a woman's level that she shouldn't go in there alone with this man. Not wearing this skirt, no matter how nice he seemed. She gave him a smile and then turned around. The house wasn't so far behind them and the sunlight was lighting it up. She really did need curtains, she could easily see in half the windows. If they'd come a little earlier, or if she'd slept a little later, she would have given all the men a free show.

But more than that—if she could see into the house—then *he* could see out. She thought she could feel his eyes on her, and she realized she wanted to be with him again.

She turned back toward Luke. "I have to go back."

"You don't want to see the workshop on the second floor?"

"Maybe another time."

He looked surprised, but nodded. "Of course."

"I may try my hand at the herb garden before you return."

"If you need any seeds or starters, let me know." He smiled warmly and she felt it radiate through her, like the rays of the rising sun, but nowhere near as hot as the Master's hands.

ARTHUR WAS THERE every time she turned around that day. She'd be reaching seductively inside of a box, the door would open, and he'd be there. Now that the library was finished, he needed a lot more guidance to help, which normally she wouldn't mind, only she had a ghost to seduce.

When she thought about it that way, it became completely ludicrous and she couldn't help but smile and shake her head, Arthur trailing her down the hall.

"I found something I think you should see, Ma'am," he announced on the fourth of his interruptions.

"Really?" She looked around the room. She hadn't felt him watching her yet. Was he? Or was he distracted, too?

"I think you'll be pleased."

"All right." She dusted her hands against her skirt in an unladylike fashion. "Lead on."

ARTHUR TOOK her to the closet of one of the back bedrooms and opened the door up dramatically. "See?"

There was a large box on the ground, and in it were bolts of fabric. She knelt down and picked one up. "Are these what I think they are?"

"I believe so! Curtains!"

"Oh thank God. I didn't know how we were going to get anyone to come out here to measure things, or how long they'd take to make." She held the top one up. They were a drab grey, but it didn't matter.

"I'd assumed they'd taken them, and were going to hem them for their new home. I had no idea this was here."

"Well, this isn't enough to do all the windows, not unless you find another box or ten. But these will do the bedroom just fine—and we can take our time working on the rest."

"I'll start steaming the creases out this afternoon."

Daphne rose to standing, beaming at him. One more step in getting this house into shape. Her house. Her wonderful, amazing house. "You were right, Arthur. These are delightful."

He bowed politely with a broad grin on his face. "Thank you, Ma'am."

SHE CONTINUED to unpack for the rest of the day. Richard would have to send her somewhere to buy more things, or they'd have to shutter half the bedrooms off.

The feeling of being watched, that she'd had this morning while outside, was gone now, and she didn't know what to make of that. What if he'd gone away? Maybe he could only appear near a full moon? She didn't know how ghosts worked. It was possible, wasn't it?

And so as dinner passed and there was still no sign of him, her anticipation curdled into fear. What if Arthur and Mrs. Dudley left tonight, and she was in her newly curtained room, completely alone?

Daphne found she couldn't bear the thought.

"Is there anything else, Ma'am?" Arthur asked, after collecting the last of dinner's cutlery.

"No. Thank you." She didn't know whether to plead for him to stay to keep her company or push him out the door and pray. "I'm fine," she said, smiling, using the same calm voice she'd used with Richard on the phone, the one that anyone—if they knew her very well— would know meant that she was lying.

"Glad to hear it, Ma'am. Breakfast at eight again?"

"On the dot. See you then." She waved at him as he left the dining room and heard the alarm chirp on their way out.

SHE WAITED in the dining room after that, pensive—scared. No heat, no sensation of being watched, just the vast presence of an empty house looming over her like a squatting hen.

Daphne got up, pushed her chair in, and walked out to the hall. If there was anywhere that he was likely to be, it was her bedroom, surely. He must be waiting for her there. He simply must.

She walked slowly, preparing for the best and the worst simultaneously, feeling her clit throb with each step. She needed him to take care of her, to make her feel alive again—and she realized she didn't know what she would do in this huge empty house without him. Go insane, probably.

Daphne placed her foot on the first stair up to her wing of the second floor—and was yanked back, from behind.

CHAPTER 7

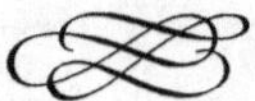

*H*eat covered all of her, her back, her ass, her neck. Hands molested her roughly over her clothing, mauling her breasts, pushing through the fabric of her skirt to grope at her crotch. She cried out in fear and relief—he was still here, he'd been waiting for her after all—and he threw her to the cold tile.

She caught herself only barely, on all fours—in the morning there'd be bruises on her knees. A hand she couldn't see wound in her hair and pulled her head back as another hand pushed up her skirt and yanked down her underwear, and she knew what he had planned —he was going to ride her like a horse, right here in the entry-way hall.

Daphne felt the heat of him behind her, covering her ass and thighs, and then he let go of her hair and pushed her forward, buckling her down so that her ass was higher than the rest. She felt him pull her buttocks wide as if he were inspecting her—and she knew she was already ready for him, hopelessly, shamefully wet.

With one solid plunge he pushed his hot spear of a cock inside.

She cried out again as it rammed into her, in hunger and surprise. He started taking her roughly, right from the start, fucking her—on the cold tile there was no such thing as consideration, or as love. She scrabbled to hold onto something, anything, but the tile had no give and his cock was relentless, taking her hard and fast and deeply.

She didn't want to come for him like this, dirtily spread apart, given no choice in the matter, but her body betrayed her and she felt her pussy begin to clench. She fought to hold on, to hold off, to not give him the satisfaction while keeping all of it in for herself, but she couldn't—the hammering of his cock and the titillating shame of the situation shoved her over the edge.

She cried out again and it echoed through the house's empty halls, making it sound like a howl instead of a shout, and she felt her pussy lock down on him, milking him as hard as it could in her wild orgasm. She shouted again, feeling all of him inside of her, brilliantly hard and straight and hot, and then sagged to the ground, barely cupping her hands in front of her face for the fall.

He took three more long strokes, still impossibly hard, owning her pussy just because he could and then pulled back, freeing her from his cock. Her hips dropped to the floor and she lay there, dizzy and gasping, her own juices seeping wetly from her cunt—that's what it was now, she thought, after he'd used it like that—to stain the front of her skirt.

The sensation of heat from behind her disappeared, and Daphne realized she could maybe stay there all night, except that the tile was cold.

DAPHNE MADE her way upstairs after taking off her low heels and got into her bedroom, half expecting a repeat performance the second she walked in. But no one waited for her there—and without his heat surrounding her, she found herself chilly.

She got undressed and dropped her clothes to the ground and made her way into the bathroom's claw-footed tub and drew the shower curtain closed.

Would he come for her again tonight? Would she, in turn, come again for him? She should be too tired to think of such things, or too scared—or angry that he'd had his way with her downstairs, like that, just taken her in the hall—but as the water sluiced down her naked body it washed away her exhaustion, her impropriety, her shame. She'd wanted someone to use her—anyone—and if she were completely honest with herself, she'd enjoyed being used.

She rinsed her hair off and began the work of washing off her body. Reaching down for the soap and coming up again she paused with a gasp.

Outside the milky white shower curtain, she could see a form. Her heart started beating faster, fear and hope twining again. Did he know she could see him? He was taller than her, but she couldn't tell what he looked like. Was that for the best? Could he see her, in here? She swallowed, picking the soap up.

She cleaned herself off with him watching. Her boldness returned to her and it became a game, much as unpacking had. She held one arm up just so and faced him, while she washed off her left breast, and then repeated the show on the other side, taking elaborate care as her hands slid down her body, putting pointed toes up on the edge of the tub as she soaped and rinsed herself off, until the only space left to clean was that one, the one he'd just fucked.

There was no way to make washing her pussy off sexy, and so she didn't try. She just stood there, facing him, hidden by the shower curtain, reaching with soapy fingers between her folds, and then cupping water with both hands to rinse herself off.

She bent over to set the soap down—and when she came up again, he was gone.

Daphne dried herself off in the bathroom and pulled her robe on. She reached out for the door knob and rested her hand on it without turning. She had no idea what—if anything—would be waiting for her outside, and she found that she liked not knowing and being scared.

She turned the handle and stepped out into her boudoir.

There was a divot on her sheets, as though a man sat on the edge of her bed. She walked across the room to him, discarding her robe. She felt more powerful naked than she ever had wearing clothes.

Daphne presented herself. Because he couldn't speak, she couldn't know what he wanted—he'd have to show her with his hands. One hot hand grabbed her wrist and pulled her closer—and a hot arm pulled her awkwardly down.

"What?" she fought, then remembered if she pushed through him, she'd break the illusion they shared, that he had all the power. She felt his legs beneath her stomach, her naked breasts jiggling on the far side of his thighs as her ass—for the second time that night—went in the air. She was like a poor 1950's housewife or a recalcitrant school-girl, about to feel a father's wrath.

Before she could protest further, or ask what was going on, the first blow landed. She felt the heat of it, the weight of it, as it stung her with pain and surprise. It reverberated through her, body and soul. Was this really happening? Was she letting it happen to her? She had an infinity of time to contemplate exactly how she had gotten here before she felt the next smack.

"No—" she protested, as the heat flooded her again. It welled up from his hands as he hit her, from legs beneath her, and she could feel the bobbing of his hot cock against her stomach. If she were honest with herself, she felt the heat rising from between her own legs. "Stop—"

Another smack. There would be no stopping, at least not on her behalf. The ghost would continue until he saw fit, and she would just have to learn how to take it.

He changed his hand so that his next spank was a slap, crisply echoing around the room, and he began to speed up, striking one spot repeatedly before changing to the other, cooler, cheek. His handprints weren't differentiated on her anymore, they were like an endless stream that blended together, and she was squirming, squirming, squirming to get away from them, twisting in his lap to hide herself from him, but unable to get away. Her body genuinely wanted flight, but her mind needed his attention and knew—hoped, prayed—that he wouldn't give her more than she could take, although with each new strike she felt closer to crying for mercy than the last and ending their game—assuming he would stop then.

Just as she thought she couldn't take anymore, that her bottom was on ruined, that she'd never recover—he stopped.

She tensed on his lap, unable to believe it was over, oddly missing it now that it was gone. Her head was spinning, she didn't know what to think, she'd used her riding crop on horses before, but she'd never had anyone else put her through her paces—not like that.

He stroked a hand over her wet hair and down her back and softly, so softly, over the ass he'd just welted. She whimpered and twitched, an animal sound, feeling small and lost. He stroked her again, calm, and reassuring. The man whose hands cared for her like that, who touched her so gently after bruising her—surely there were bruises— she didn't know what to make of him anymore.

His hands reached down the backs of her thighs, to the back of her knees, and then back up more slowly. She was worried that he was coming again for her ass and she tensed—then felt him push his way between her thighs, still involuntarily clenched to protect her pussy from his prior onslaught. Nervous yet hoping, even if she couldn't have put that hope into words—she opened her legs slightly and let him in.

Hot fingers pushed inside of her ever so easily. She was wet again, even after having washed herself off in the shower, the rain of blows he'd landed on her ass had turned her on in spite of herself. His fingers moved inside of her, sliding in and out, and she moaned.

The pain was over now. She knew somehow she'd tolerated it— ridden it, like it was an animal—and come out the other side. Which meant now it was time for pleasure.

He brought his wet fingers out and circled her clit, before pushing them into her again. He made a game of it, of teasing her like this, stirring his heat against her pussy's walls, until it felt maddeningly good, only to pull out and pay attention to her clit. And then he'd rub her own wetness over her, pushing on her slow and hard, too hard almost, until she was too sensitive to stand it and needed things faster with less pressure, then plunging his fingers into her pussy again.

She had no idea how long they were there, the blood rushing to her breasts and head, her slung across his lap, dizzy from the pain and hope. She reached a hand up to pull at one of her nipples and moaned, feeling the electricity jolt down to where his fingers were once again teasing her clit.

She rolled her nipples between her fingers, holding the heavy weight of her breasts, letting his lap completely support her—feeling the heat of his hard cock stroke against her belly. She moved a hand awkwardly up, trying to reach for him, and got one swift strike on her already raw bottom in return for it. She whimpered and she would've sworn she could feel him move as though he were chuckling.

He wanted control—and so she let him have it. She rubbed her own breasts, feeling the delicious softness of her own skin, as he manipulated her at his leisure. She whined and she moaned and—over everything else—she gave in. Her hips thrust against his lap and back into his hand and his fingers lazily circled her clit then sped faster as she moaned anew.

She was going to come soon and both of them knew it. Hot fingers pressed faster, pushed deeper inside, and she panted, suspended, breasts in her hands, nipples pinched hard.

"Oh—oh—oh—" she began, searching for a word to call him, to name him for what he'd done—she lit on Arthur's term and before she could think twice shouted, "Master—I'm coming—I'm coming!" at the top of her lungs.

His hand didn't stop until she did, collapsed across his lap like a cat. He pulled his fingers out of her, and one more time he stroked her back. Then he moved beneath her and she slid to the ground, leaning against the bed for strength. Heat brushed her face, her thighs, and then disappeared, leaving her alone again.

DAPHNE WOKE to the ringing of the house's landline phone at five AM. She rolled back onto the bed, stiff from sleeping on her side all night, and discovered why she had done so—her bottom was raw.

The phone wasn't a figment of her imagination though. She stumbled up to standing like a fawn, between the heat of her ass and the soreness of her pussy, and staggered down the hall.

"Hello?" It had to be Richard, he was the only one who had the number.

"Daphne!"

"Who else would it be?" she said, a subtle dig.

"I'm sorry to wake you, pet, I've gone and forgotten what time it is there."

"I think it's five."

"Never too soon to let you know I'm coming home early—they cancelled the extra days."

"Really? Why?" She leaned carefully against the wall behind the phone. It was cold, it felt good on her bottom.

"Because I couldn't stand the thought of you doing all that unpacking without me."

Daphne licked her lips in thought—she wished she could believe him. "Do you know when?"

"Tomorrow. I want to see everything you've done. Especially the bedroom, if you know what I mean."

"I always do, Richard, don't I?" she said.

"I love you, pet."

"I love you, Richard," she said back, out of habit, and hung up the phone.

ONE MORE DAY, and he'd be home. All because she'd caught him with that woman, and he had a guilty conscience. Guilty because it was his first time? Or guilty because he'd finally gotten caught? Daphne supposed she'd never know—even if he told her the truth, she'd have to assume he was lying to her.

As for her side of things—she slunk into the nearest bathroom, which had a much lower vanity than hers, and twisted to look at her ass in the mirror. All of her bottom was a bright cherry red. She put an experimental hand on it, and it stung—it was even still warm.

What was she going to do? She couldn't tell Richard—he didn't deserve to know. But she did need him—she needed to stay here now, this was her home. If they got divorced, he'd sell this place for sure.

And what was more, was that she did still want a child. Richard might not be a good husband, or father, but he did have a lot of funds. Private schools weren't cheap, and neither were ivy league colleges.

If she could manage to lead Richard on, to make him think they were happy, at least until she got pregnant…then things might be okay, mightn't they? There was no way he'd stay home, he'd go away again on a business trip, philandering—and when he was gone, she would have the baby and the ghost. The best of all possible worlds, right?

She stroked the curve of her ass, watching her hand in the mirror. Yes. If she could keep her wits about her, it just might be possible to juggle it all.

She unpacked with a vengeance that day, no flouncing or posing. She wanted Richard to feel bad when he got home when he saw how much she'd done, toiling away without him. Arthur brought up boxes and they shoved furniture around as a team, until all the bedrooms on her wing were done. She'd already picked out one of them to be her nursery—all they had to do was get one of the dressers the locusts had left behind out the door.

It was heavy wood, an ancient piece, she could understand why the locusts had left it behind. It was far too grim for a nursery though—it had to be moved.

"Let's put our backs into it, Arthur —"

"Ma'am, my back may not have much more left to give!" Arthur said with a laugh.

But the felt beneath the dresser's feet suddenly glided across the floor and they slid it out the door and down the hall to the spare room Daphne was using to hide all the furniture she didn't want or need.

They both walked back up the hall slowly, hands to backs, congratulating each other on a job well done, returning to the newly empty room. The walls were the wrong color—mint green, whereas she'd want pink or blue, child depending—but the windows were shaded by tall trees outside, letting in the perfect amount of light.

Her eyes scanned the room, imagining her future life, when she lit on a dusty photo tilted against the wall where the dresser had been. She walked over and picked it up.

It was of a woman holding up a trophy in front of a giant black horse.

"Who's this?"

Arthur came over to look over her shoulder. "I believe that was one of the prior tenant's children."

Children? She wasn't a child. Daphne squinted, and saw it, the innocence around the eyes—but the curves of her body, shown off by the tight breeches and top she wore, were all woman.

"She's beautiful."

"Indeed. It was a shame."

She turned towards him, a question in her eyes.

"She's the one that died," he explained.

"So—this was her room?"

"I believe so."

Daphne frowned. This house was only big enough for one ghost. "I think we'll have to move the nursery down the hall."

Arthur nodded. "A wise decision, Ma'am."

She waited until the alarm chirped that night, and addressed the ghost directly, knowing he had to hear.

"My husband's coming home tomorrow. You can't do—*that*—again," she told thin air. Was he in the room, hovering in quiet disapproval? Or was she only projecting her own disappointment out? "I'm sorry. I," she began and licked her lips, scared to say the words aloud, especially when the ghost could never say them back.

A warm finger touched the cool space of her arm. Forgiveness? She turned towards him. "I really do—" She'd had all day to think on it when she'd been alone, in between unpacking things. It was so scary to say things out loud, to say what she needed—her whole life she'd been conditioned to never ask for what she wanted, always praying that somehow she'd be good enough for it to just fall in her lap.

But because he was silent, she felt the need to fill the space up between them with words—and because he couldn't talk back, talking felt safe. He would never tell a soul the way she'd writhed against him, trying to get away from him while secretly wanting more, to see how much she could take. She'd been scared, and it'd hurt, but—she ran another hand down her ass, feeling the soreness he'd left behind, feeling claimed by him in a way that Richard hadn't wanted her in years. "I—I think you should know that—I liked it."

A warm hand took hers, palm to palm, and pulled her towards the entry hall and her breath hitched to think he might take her there again, like that, but instead of pushing her down, or pulling her towards the stairs that led to her bedroom, he tugged her gently towards the other stairs instead.

Curious, scared—*excited*—she followed.

CHAPTER 8

She and Arthur hadn't gotten very far on this side of the house. All her bedroom furniture had been concentrated on the other side, what she thought of as the 'living' wing—which perhaps made it more appropriate that she was here on the other side with the ghost of someone who'd died here.

As he pulled her further down the hallway, she thought she knew where they'd end up, and something low in her belly quivered. The bed, the manly bed, carved with fighting animals, abandoned by the locusts—he drew her to the room inexorably and with every step, knowing only enough about what was to come to be turned on and scared at once, she felt the ache of desire rekindle within her. There were spaces in her that only he could fill, that needed filling, desperately. She knew if she reached down now she'd find herself wet and knew she ought to be ashamed of how eager he made her and yet knowing he was going to take her soon felt so good.

They reached the door of the room and turned into it. She reached for the lightswitch, but he held her hand back, and a soft glow suffused the room instead. Candlelight, but from no one point, just a gentle orange glow, centered on the four poster bed.

The color of the light returned the bare mattress to its former glory, making it look warm and inviting, shadows hiding the anger of the animals carved to hold it up beneath.

Of course the hand drew her there.

She walked slowly, her belly on fire. *It's about to happen again, to me, to me, to me,* her thoughts kept pace with her steps. When she reached the bed's edge, the hand held her back and began to undress her.

She stood there, feeling him move gently over her, heat pressing against her skin, pulling her shirt up and off, unzipping and tugging her skirt down for her to step out of. There was a pause, as though the ghost admired his own handiwork—or her—before hot hands undid the clasp of her bra and set her breasts free, pulling her back into a warm chest again as hands fondled her, lifting the weight of each breast up, rolling nipples between thumb and forefinger indulgently. She purred at his touch and his slow attention, then felt a hand play down her side, her ribs, to tuck a finger into the band of her underwear and pull along the elastic edge as if testing its strength. Both hands sank, pushing her underwear off of her, feeling her as they did so, following the underwear down against her legs all the way to the ground. She stepped out of them and her skirt and then felt hands again, at her waist, and stroking her welted bottom, just like they had at the end of last night. Her breath caught with each movement of his hand—she didn't think he'd spank her again, but he might—there was another rumbling behind her, as though the ghost were chuckling at her fear.

Then the heat abandoned her. She knew he was still in the room, the 'light' was still on—and she saw divots appear in the mattress, as though someone were crossing it toward her on their knees. Hands grabbed hers again, and pulled her up.

She followed the ghost on all fours, hungry and unsure. Hands pressed down on her back and she let them, falling forward like he'd taken her on the tile the other night, but then he pressed down on her ass, pushing all of her to lay prone. She did as his hands told her without complaint. Whatever he wanted her to do, she would.

His hands smoothed through her hair, pushing it back from her face, so that she had a view of the bottom of the bed and its posters. Which was how she saw it, and why she screamed—

"Snakes!" She writhed on the bed, trying to escape but a heavy weight held her down, stronger than she was like this, unable to get a purchase on the mattress.

But when her panic calmed down, she realized they were ropes.

"What?" She still fought, but not as hard as she had been. "But—"

But hadn't she come here of her own accord? Hadn't she let him undress her, knowing, hoping, something like this might occur?

She stilled beneath his hands and he stroked her again, as though to calm her down.

Ropes she could see tied down both her arms, and ropes she couldn't bound her ankles. They pulled tight and she was lashed to the bed, spread-eagled out, entirely reliant on a man she couldn't even visualize.

"Please—" she didn't want to mention her husband again, it would feel disrespectful to the moment. "Please—don't hurt me."

Not in ways that Richard could see.

But in other ways…she swallowed, and closed her eyes.

His hands smoothed all over her body again, even unexpected places, the bottoms of her feet, her armpits, the angles of her neck, like he was currying a favored horse. She relaxed under this onslaught of attention, fear of him and fear of getting caught receding. She was still hungry, yes, but she didn't dare raise her hips up as he stroked down her back, no matter how much, cat-like, she wanted to—she didn't dare invite another spanking.

And then, like she was hoping, like she'd been ready for ever since his hands had led her down this hall—his fingers began trailing up the insides of her thighs again.

There was no way to hide herself from him, tied out like she was. He could see all of her, her clit, her folds, her pussy, and, she realized, as he pulled warm cheeks apart, her tight tight asshole. She quivered in fear at this, at being so exposed. No one had ever looked at her like this before, had inspected her so thoroughly with eyes and hands, no one had ever wanted to know her so intimately, especially not like this.

His hands kneaded her ass gently and she whined—there were bruises back there now, she knew, and not all of the heat was his, she'd felt like she'd been sitting on a sunburn the entire day. Then fingers dropped lower, to test the wetness of her pussy.

"Please," she breathed, wanting him in her—any part of him, and now she arched, begging him to fill her up. Hot fingers played in and out, broad strokes, making her groan—and then moan, when they pulled out. "Please?" she said, hoping to feel the mattress shift, to know he was kneeling above her, about to use his cock.

And then a finger pressed there, hot and wet, at the tight pucker of her asshole.

"No," she said, squirming on the bed like she had on his lap the night before. The finger followed her squirming, neither pressing harder, nor going away.

"No—not even Richard—" she gasped out, all of her clenching tight in fear.

But not even Richard had ever spanked her, either. And not-even-Richard wasn't here—he was off with some other woman.

But most important of all—the Master was not him.

She paused, gulping in huge breaths, trying to conquer her fear. The ghost had hurt her yes—but he'd also pleased her, moreso than any other man ever had—had ever even bothered to try.

Daphne licked her lips and dropped her hips to the bed, took in a deep breath, and let it go.

"Be slow. Please be slow."

Instead of instantly pushing in, he rubbed her there. Now that she wasn't frightened of him, or this, she could realize that it felt good. A warm finger circled her, massaging this part of her as he had the rest of her, getting her to fall back into that blissful relaxed state—except now she was sure there was more coming. Instead of being scared of it, she began to be excited by the idea.

Time passed. Him waiting, rubbing, and her being rubbed. Daphne supposed ghosts had no concept of time, and his cock was always hard, so there was no need to hurry. And so, when she was ready, when she wanted it—at least to try it—she perked up her ass ever so slowly.

Taking the cue, he pushed his finger in.

It was strange and frightening and she locked down again. But he waited there patiently until she relaxed. She realized the sensation inside of her was strange…but pleasurable. She moved a little testing things, and he moved with her—and then against her, sliding his finger in and out.

Daphne gasped at this, but not in pain. More heat rose in her pussy and her clit begged for her to wrestle a hand free to touch it and she rocked her hips against his hand. The bed shook for a second, him chuckling to see her come alive beneath him, as his fingers moved again.

When he put a second one in, she noticed, but didn't mind. The sensation of being stretched wider was as pleasurable in her ass as it was in her pussy, and she was fucking the bed now, her hips begging him for more friction, her clit aching for relief.

And then when the whole bed shook and the fingers removed she knew what was coming next.

"Yes—" she begged in the moment he left her empty. "Please," she panted into the mattress, making her face hot.

His heat lowered on top of her, his weight pressing her down, and she felt the heat of his cock align with the cleft of her ass cheeks and she knew he was ready to take her, as ready as she was to be taken— his hips moved and with an arc and a thrust he slid his cock where his fingers had been, into her.

Daphne cried out in triumph, surprise, and a tiny bit of pain. His cock was longer than his fingers had been, wider, and hotter too, and yet having him in her ass felt right. She cried out again as he thrust into her a second time, experimentally, trying to get a feel for her as she tried to stretch for him—and then they moved as one and she groaned.

He was fucking her and she was helping him, their hips mated in a dance, moving back and forth with one another, only the smallest amount of friction between them as each claimed their rightful space.

She had absolutely never felt like this, so owned by another. It was dirty, letting him take her like this, fucking her asshole, but it felt so good—good wives didn't want this, but she wasn't a good wife anymore, was she?

Maybe good wives were only as good as their husbands.

She threw her head back and felt his arms wrap around her chest and neck, holding her tightly to him so that he could fuck her more deeply, pounding her hips into the mattress's springs. A hand reached down and grabbed her breast, pinching her nipple roughly, which only made the need of her clit roar.

"One hand, please—please—please —" she begged in time with their rhythm, her voice rising as he sped up. He could take her like this forever, she realized—how long could she stand it, before the heat made her catch fire?

It was his hand he moved—not hers. One dove beneath her, reaching down to cup near her clit—forcing her to choose.

Would she raise her ass and let him pound it? Or would she lower it and rub against him? It was a devil's bargain when both things felt so good. She screamed because she could, as the friction of her clit against his hand made her momentarily go insane—and then his other arm kept yanking her down, and himself up, opening her ass to ram in his cock—

There was no thinking anymore, no past, no future, only the present, right here on this bed with him, in this beastial fuck, getting taken like she'd never been taken before, him in complete control, riding her like a mustang running toward a cliff—

Her voice increased in volume and went hoarse. "Fuck me!" she commanded him, once the horse, now the rider. "Fuck me hard!" she demanded, and he did, his cock plumbing the dark depths of her and his hand shuddering against her clit and then—

She came. It was like she'd stepped off of cliff, and instead of falling, flown. The ecstasy didn't ripple through her, it spun out like a galaxy, emanating from her hips out through every part of her, holding her up as she slowly spun. She took in huge gulps of air hovering, floating, all of her light, his hand still rubbing and his cock still deep inside and her still coming, coming, coming, until she was done.

"Oh my God," she whispered, as the bed felt real again. He stopped touching her clit, released her shoulders, and slowly pulled out. She swallowed, still trying to hold onto the last moments of bliss, trying to convince herself that that—that this—had happened to her. That the whole thing had been real.

"I just—" she started, trying to, what exactly? Explain it to herself? Or the ghost?

The ropes binding her released and disappeared. She lay still without them, unable to catch her breath.

A gentle hand found her back, as if to ask if she were alive.

"That was amazing." She got to all fours and sat back. She'd be sore tomorrow in places she'd never been sore before—and it'd all been so very, very, worthwhile. "I can't believe…." Words drifted, thoughts incomplete.

A hand pulled her chin up and hot lips kissed hers with no tongue, the chastity a strange counterpart to what had just gone on. And then the sensation of heat, his presence, and the candlelight, disappeared.

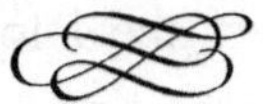

CHAPTER 9

The next morning, most of the marks on her ass were gone, and those that remained could be blamed on a fall down the stairs—the same fall that she'd say claimed her knees. She dressed conservatively and didn't feel the ghost's presence at all, which was probably easier on them both.

Richard came home around mid-day—accidentally setting the alarm off. The entire house shrieked as if in protest at his arrival, and she and Arthur ran to the entry way hall.

"Oh pet, my love, let me look at you," Richard said, flinging his bags to the ground. He always made a production of his returns, sometimes she felt like that was half the reason he left, so that he could return home the conquering hero. Arthur picked up the bags while Richard pulled her close. She could smell his aftershave and feel the tickle of a sixteen-hour-long-flight beard against her brow. "I missed you so much."

"I missed you too," she said, realizing as she did so that it was a lie.

She had been taken on the very tile they now stood together on. She'd been forced onto her knees, head down, ass up, and she'd been fucked until her pussy had come around another man's cock. Daphne forced a smile up at him. "How was Tokyo?"

"Miserable. Everywhere is miserable without you."

She shook her head. Her lies, she could stomach, his, not so much. "That's laying it on a little thick, Richard."

"What, I'm not allowed to miss my wife?" He pinched her ass and she jumped as the ghost's bruises stung. "Show me what you've unpacked—starting with the bedroom," he said, beginning to grope at her.

Daphne remembered when she'd looked forward to these days, him mauling her when he came home, how their lovemaking then made all the absences worthwhile. She hadn't known then that he was merely searching for absolution after his indiscretions. But now that she had indiscretions of her own—and she needed this house and she wanted a child—she grabbed his hand and pulled him up the stairs.

THEY WERE both putting on a performance for the other, like a school talent show. Him the loving husband, her the loving wife, both knowing they were pretending, desperately hoping the other one wouldn't catch on. He threw his suit jacket and tie to the floor, while she wriggled out of jeans and pulled up her shirt.

He stopped unbuttoning his shirt at the sight of her knees. "What're those from?"

"I tripped and fell. You should see my ass—" she explained.

"I should see your ass all right," he growled, and crossed the bedroom to her.

Richard was bigger than she was. She'd always liked that about him, how it always seemed like he was stronger than her. She knew differently now—could he have taken the ghost's paddling? Sat there and accepted it, worked through the pain and come out whole on the far side?—but when he picked her up and threw her onto their bed she didn't fight. He yanked her underwear down, leaving her bra and his undershirt and pants on and mounted up, like he wanted inside her so bad he couldn't wait.

For her part, the clothing between them became part of her armor. He wasn't touching all of her, there were parts of her he couldn't see.

And so when his erection nudged between her legs, thrusting at her dry pussy she still felt like her own being. She would give this small part of her over, the part that lived between her legs, but the rest of her remained her own—and the Master's.

Richard groaned as his tip pushed inside her. He was having to push hard and getting off on that. He kissed her roughly, for his sake, not hers, hoping that she would loosen, that her walls would let down and juices would flow. He pulled out and tried again, shoved in only a fraction of an inch further.

"Come on now," Richard whispered.

"You're going so fast—" she said, like she was turned on.

He grit his teeth, pulled out, and pushed in again and she panted. It hurt, but, some traitor part of her was getting turned on. He stroked the head of his cock in and out with what little lubrication there was until a dam broke inside of her, wetness flowed, and he could thrust in her freely.

He groaned, sliding home, and she exhaled in a rush, and together they began to rock on the bed, his cock in her pussy, locked in a familiar dance. She clutched her hands in the back of his shirt, holding on as he took her desperately, looking for forgiveness in the sex, trying to plow it into her, attempting to prove his devotion.

And Daphne closed her eyes and let her head roll back and thought of another man, one she couldn't quite see. With each pant out she thought, "The house." And with each groan in, she thought, "A baby."

She wound her hands tighter, pulling him closer to her so their lips couldn't touch, so she was breathing into his shoulder, as his hips started to spasm and his cock got rock hard—and he moaned over her, shouting out, ramming his seed deep inside her where she prayed it took—thrusting a few halfhearted moments more before pulling out and falling to lay beside her on the bed.

"I'm sorry pet—I want you to come too—I just needed you so bad, and you're so hot right now and I missed you." Words burbled out of him just as cum leaked out of her, she could feel the wet heat of it seeping between her thighs.

"That's okay," she said. "I wanted you too," she lied.

WHEN SHE GOT out of the shower, Richard was waiting in his robe, holding hers out to her. "Come on, pet, I want to get the tour."

"But," she protested. Robes seemed awfully familiar. "Arthur's downstairs working, and this is the only room that has curtains."

"We're paying Arthur—he can look the other way. And curtains—who cares? There's no one out for miles to look in." Richard shook the robe. "Come on, I want to see my property."

Daphne took the robe and forced a grin. "Okay."

SHE TOOK him through the upstairs first, and showed him the room—not the green one—that she wanted for a nursery. Then she showed him the other wing, with its massive final bedroom, and the piano waiting for a child to want to play.

Then they walked down through the assorted living areas of downstairs. She knew the ghost was watching her—that or guilt was prickling her neck at every turn.

And then they wound up in the library.

Richard made an approving noise at seeing his neatly alphabetized books, but frowned back at the portrait staring down from above the fireplace. He leaned against the massive desk that, along with a couch, was the library's only other furniture, and shook his head at the portrait.

"That has got to go," he said.

"What?" She'd been looking at the shelves where the ghost had ravished her after her realization of Richard's betrayal. Would the ghost think she was betraying him, now?

"That painting. It's hideous."

Daphne drew up straight. "It is not. It's an antique. It's part of the house's history."

Richard gave her a disbelieving look. "I thought you had more taste than that, pet."

"I think it goes perfectly well in here. The shelves even go around it—if we take it down, it'll look out of place."

"We can fix the shelves, or hang another portrait. One of me, perhaps," he said, sliding his hand into his robe in the style of Napoleon. Daphne snorted.

"Or just leave that one there, where it belongs."

Richard opened his mouth to say one more thing. He hardly ever gave her ground, but this time he closed his mouth again and shrugged.

In its own way it was one more small sign that he'd cheated on her.

THEY BOTH GOT DRESSED for dinner that night, Arthur presented it right at seven, and they sat across from one another, as though they were out on the town.

"So," Daphne began, holding her glass of wine conversationally. "How was Tokyo?"

Cutting a piece of steak, Richard paused in thought.

Times like these she thought she could actually see the calculations running behind his eyes. He was a banker, he couldn't help himself.

"Hot. Miserable. Certain investments we'd made there've dried up —the firm's pissed off. International things always have a large amount of risk involved—different cultures, different ideas." He shook his head, bringing his fork up, staring her directly in the eyes. "It was a bad idea and a waste of time. I won't be going back."

Daphne pursed her lips. Even if she were to press Richard for a million years, that might be the only admission of guilt she ever got— and also the only apology.

"Never again?" she asked, torn, and feeling small.

"Never." He planted the bite of steak into his mouth and chewed vengefully.

AFTER DINNER, Richard excused himself and Daphne followed him upstairs. They got ready for bed like they always did while he was in town, brushing their teeth beside each other in the sink, and she saw him reach into his shaving kit for a prescription bottle.

"Sorry pet—I know you were hoping for another round, but I've been up for two days straight, what with travel and fighting jet-lag," he explained, pouring a pill out into his palm. "I'm scared I'll go to bed for three hours and then wake up at dawn on Japan time."

"It's all right, that makes sense," she said, watching him swallow it. Each with pajamas on, they crawled into bed for the night.

DAPHNE LAY there for an hour listening to him breathe. His weight in the bed felt good, as did his heat, and the way he'd reach out for her if she rolled too far away. When he was sleeping it was easier to remember what she loved about him and the way it used to be.

She was almost asleep herself when she felt the covers on the bed shift in the dark, as though someone were joining them. She opened her mouth up in a gasp, and felt it covered by a hot hand.

She could breathe through the hand, it was a reminder, not a punishment—but even if she could speak, what should she say? That there a ghost was in the bed, haunting them? Even if she woke Richard up right now he wouldn't believe her.

Instead she arched back a little, feeling the heat of the ghost press up against her back—and one warm hand dart between her thighs. She bit her lips not to cry out as he started rubbing her there, right beside her husband's sleeping form.

The heat of him pressed against her, the illicit nature of it all, the fact that his hand was circling her clit—she started breathing in hot gasps, immeasurably turned on.

But it was wrong. Richard was here. She should want to be with him. He was sorry for what he'd done, he'd said as much at dinner that night—and only Richard could give her a baby.

She shook herself free of the ghost's embrace, and the ghost didn't fight her.

"Richard—" She pushed her own hand down to keep what the

ghost had started in her warm. "Richard, wake up—I need you —wake up—"

She moved her hand over him and reached down into his boxers, finding his flaccid cock there, stroking it with desire. "Richard," she whispered, begging him.

His hands pushed her roughly away. "Too tired, Becca. Go."

Daphne let herself be pushed back in quiet horror. Becca. Who was Becca? How long had there been a Becca? Was she another secretary?

She lay in bed quietly beside him, impotent tears streaming down her face. Who was Becca? Where was Becca?

She felt sick to her stomach and went into the bathroom to throw up.

CHAPTER 10

"Why?" she asked the mirror quietly. She'd been so good, up until this past week. She'd tried so hard, despite all the absences—God, what if he was living a separate life? What if instead of going off to international places, he was getting on a plane and flying to see another family? Someone else who thought she was his wife, with three children? Maybe *she* was the other family, and that other one was his 'real' one?

She sank to the tile of the bathroom floor, sobbing quietly—and after a moment felt hot fingers on her cheeks, stroking away her tears.

"I'm so sorry," she told him. "I don't mean to be like this."

The Master's presence around her calmed her, and she leaned into his heat like a cat.

"You've never lied to me," she whispered. "I wish—I wish there were some way I could repay you. You keep giving to me and it seems like there's nothing that I can give to you—" She licked her lips and opened them, trying to think of some way to pay the ghost back—and then it occurred to her. "Take my mouth. Right now. Like this. Use me how you want to." She carefully opened her mouth wide in mid-air.

Hot hands pushed through her hair winding it to the point that it pulled—and then she felt heat slide inside her mouth in the shape of a cock.

The ghost was hesitant at first, but it didn't last long.

She closed her eyes and gave into it, anything else would have been creepy. With her eyes closed she could feel his hands in her hair and his cock in her mouth, pursing her lips against its warm length, tasting the smooth perfection of it pushing in and out, the head of him bobbing at the back of her throat, her face buried in the heat of his belly as she almost gagged—he rocked her back and forth on him, like she was a see-saw and she brought her hands up to clutch for support and found sizzlingly hot buttocks clenched, thrusting forward. They felt so real she opened blinked her eyes open—

When the door opened up instead.

"What's wrong?" Richard asked, finding her kneeling on the floor, her hair wild.

Daphne closed her mouth, her jaw sore and fell forward. "I—I spilled some water," she quickly lied, miming wiping it up.

"Let Arthur get it tomorrow—I have something for you now," he growled while reaching down.

He took her arm same as the ghost had and led her back to bed, lying back in the dark. "I had a dream you attacked me—that you wanted this." He pulled her hand down so that it touched his cock again, now completely hard.

That was before Becca, she wanted to protest. But the house, and the baby, and the house—his hands reached for her hips and she didn't fight him as he pulled her clothes off. She kicked out of her underwear and felt him lift her up, pulling her to rest on top of him. She straddled him and his erection and felt him slide home. She moaned as he chuckled to find her already so wet. He thought it was all because of him, little did he know—she raised her hips and slammed them down roughly. This had nothing to do with him. Nothing. It was all hers and no one else's, and she would use her pussy as she saw fit.

She would take what she wanted from him, now, and any other time she wanted it, but he would never have the rest of her again. She would always know, she would always be holding a little of herself off, he would never get all of her, not again, never.

She rode her frustration out on him and he groaned with every thrust, his drugged hands reached for her shoulders, just barely hanging on as she bobbed on and off of him. She licked the fingers of one hand and sent them seeking down to rub herself—she was going to take her orgasm from his cock and take his fucking cum deep inside until she'd gotten what she wanted—and after that she would never have to touch him again.

"My pet—my pet," he started to pant as she rocked hard over him and then her hand shuddered one final perfect time and she howled, anger and frustration pouring out. Her hips bucked wildly, riding his cock into the ground, and he came at this, his hands clutching her waist tight.

Daphne panted over him, her jaw still sore from the ghost earlier, knowing the ghost was watching her now, watching her be with Richard as he gave her something the ghost could not. She growled at the unfairness of everything and dismounted him, feeling him slide limply out. She fell to the mattress and put a hand to her belly.

Please, she prayed to the darkness. *Please.*

Richard growled and rolled over to pull her close. "You were like a wild thing. I've never been with anyone like you," he whispered sleepily in her ear.

More than anything else, Daphne wished she could believe him.

DAPHNE WOKE next to an empty bed shortly after dawn. She blinked and sat up. "Richard?" she said, her voice weak.

She got up and looked in the bathroom, no Richard, and so she quietly opened the door to the hall.

His voice echoed up from the landline, clear as if she were listening in herself.

"Don't you think I know that?" A pause. "I—baby—I know. I know," he said, trying to cut someone off. "I just need a week at home, okay? She needs some time with me, all right?"

Daphne swallowed dry, wondering how the woman on the far end of the line was taking that. Apparently not well, judging by how long the pause was.

"Don't be like that," Richard said, sounding offended.

Daphne rolled her eyes. At least he wasn't only a jerk to her.

A longer pause, and then the sound of a manly purr. "No. She's asleep now. I want to know. Tell me...."

No matter that his dick still smelled like her, and that she still leaked his cum. She ground her teeth together. Go down there now and snap the phone from his hand? Use the cord to garrote him?

But if he were dead, or they broke up...no house, and no baby. *Goddammit.* Why couldn't this be easy? Why should she have to choose?

The sound of a lawnmower began in the distance, and she blinked. That was right, Luke and his crew were back, getting an early start on all the acreage.

She pulled back from the doorway, Richard's death on her mind, and forced herself to be calm. She'd wait until he was done, until he tried to sneak back into bed—and then confront him. Tell him everything she knew, Tokyo, Becca, whoever it was that he was talking to now.

She strode over to the window, and peeked out through the curtain. Luke was striding across the yard, hedge clippers in hand.

Before she could think about it twice, she knocked on the glass.

He stopped, looking up at her. He squinted, and then waved. Daphne, covered mostly by the curtain, waved back.

Luke was the only man in sight right now, the rest of his crew were out operating the riding mowers that kept nature tame. He made a gesture, and took a few steps, heading for the door, thinking that she wanted to see him.

But that wasn't what she wanted at all.

What she wanted...was to be seen.

Daphne stepped out from behind the curtain. The wall of gray fabric fell closed behind her, showing her nakedness to the window's glass.

Luke stood there, transfixed. She thought he might storm away, angry, or in fear of being fired, but instead he looked up at her boldly.

Daphne leaned into the window's glass and breathed across one pane. She put her hands out and leaned forward until her nipples brushed the cold glass and went as hard as diamonds. She rose up on her toes and then down again, dragging her breasts across the glass.

Was his hand clutching onto the clippers more tightly? Did his breath catch in his chest? She wanted to know she was turning him on, was controlling him like that long-distance witch was her husband right now. Daphne leaned forward again and licked a streak up the glass, and saw Luke's jaw drop, and thought she could see the growing outline of his cock press against his jeans. She nuzzled the glass like it was a lover, and then let one of her hands down to play between her legs.

Luke took this for the invitation it was. He dropped the clippers and undid his pants to set his cock free—it was as strong and tan as him. And then he started to stroke himself for her, a show for a show.

Daphne spread her legs and dove her fingers deeper in. She didn't want to come now, she just needed to have this power over him, to watch him stroke himself. She threw her other arm up over head and pressed her breasts against the glass like she was making love to it, to him, thrusting her hips against its chill.

The more she writhed, the faster he touched himself, standing out in the open light of dawn like a misplaced Pan, stroking his cock and thrusting his hips at her, worshiping her from afar. She danced for him, turning around so that he could see her ass, bending forward so that he could see even more, her fingers still pulsing deep inside. He held his hand up to spit in it and then returned it to himself, his strokes becoming a blur.

Daphne turned back around and put one foot up on her night-stand, holding herself up with one arm and leg, letting him clearly see her sex and—more than that—her fucking herself as hard as she could for him. What started as a lark became deadly serious as tension built and need mounted and she went up on one dangerous toe—

She bit down on her lips to not scream when she came, her whole body rocking in passion, making the curtain behind her shudder. Below her, Luke's face took on the determination of a man about to come and she saw his hips begin to buck his cock into his hand. His mouth opened, and she wondered if he was screaming, or if, like her, he had to swallow it down inside. And then his shoulders fell and his hand sagged, tucking his used cock back into place.

He knelt and wiped his hand in the grass at his feet—*she'd made him come, she really had!* she realized with a thrill—and then he fastened his pants, and stared, still unafraid, straight up at her.

Then a secret smile lit up his face and he tipped an imaginary hat to her before picking up his clippers again and walking on.

Pleased as punch, she emerged from the curtains into her bedroom and crawled back beneath the sheets.

CHAPTER 11

"Iknow, pet," Richard said to her, in the same tone she'd overhead him using earlier. "But even though I'm home, it's not a weekend for me. I've got to get my computer running so that I can check the markets. I've already been off for a whole day of travelling, you know?"

Daphne nodded. She'd asked him to help her move something—she was worried about Arthur's back. Richard had been hiding in the room he'd announced was his study all day. Neither of them had said anything about last night—or this morning.

"Fucking real estate agents—fiber gigabit my ass," Richard cursed as she slowly backed out the door.

SHE RETURNED to Arthur on the second floor. "I'm sorry—"

"Ma'am, just let me help," he protested.

"We'll get to it. There's no rush. We're not going anywhere. Let's try it again tomorrow—or hire some help from in town." She thought of Luke with a flush. "Maybe we could get Mr. Sanderson to come up?"

"We could've—but I fear they've already left for the day. It seems they got an early start."

"I think so," she said, biting back a secret smile. "But if he says he'll come up later, it's okay to leave it alone until then."

"What will you be doing for the rest of the day?" Arthur inquired politely.

A string of curses echoed out from Richard's study, and Daphne sighed.

"I think I'll be taking a walk outside."

DAPHNE LET herself out the back and into the fallow vegetable garden. A few untamed cabbage were bolting, sending up wide stalks of yellow flowers, trying to hold onto their place against the surrounding weeds. She wondered how long she could keep this pretense up—how long could she swallow her pride?

If Richard would just stay home for a whole month, if he'd just fuck her once a day, if he'd just loved her like she'd loved him before she knew about any of this—she sat down on a bench and couldn't help but draw a comparison between herself and the garden in front of her, like so much perfectly tilled soil, her womanhood was going to waste.

The sun baked down on her—and then she felt an even more intense heat on her leg in the shape of one hand.

She'd almost forgotten about the ghost, between last night and hearing Richard this morning. *He* still was here for her. No matter what.

"Oh God," she began to apologize, turning towards him. She thought she could feel her shoulder brush his. "Things haven't been how I planned at all. We don't love each other anymore, it's clear, isn't it?"

The ghost didn't say anything and didn't move.

"It's just that I desperately want a child. And you can't give me that —plus if I leave him, I leave here. You don't want that either, do you?"

The hand on her leg squeezed it once.

"But I know I've been awful. Luring you in and then him interrupting, and then you watching me with him...." She didn't dare mention her time in the window at dawn. "It's just—ever since you opened me up—I've been flooded with all these wants and needs and desires." Daphne pursed her lips in thought. "I feel like I don't know who I am now. I know who I used to be, but I don't want to be her anymore." As she said the words she started to cry. The ghost looped an arm around her shoulders and pulled her close. Closing her eyes she leaned into him without fear and it was like he was there, really holding her as she sobbed.

"Everything is so hard. I don't know if I'm strong enough to handle it."

The ghost held her, and then set her straight on the bench, and disappeared.

"Wait—come back—don't go!" She didn't want to be alone yet.

A shadow was coming up—Richard? More likely Arthur, with tea. She wiped at her eyes so he wouldn't know she'd been crying, and turned and saw no one there. She looked again at the shadow, stretched long by the angle of the sun. Was that the man she was with right now? A sudden movement attracted her eyes—and she saw a stick moving, held up in front of the wall of shrubs that shielded the garden. A cane.

She'd wondered aloud if she was strong—and so he'd gone and found a way to prove it to her.

Daphne swallowed and stood. It made all the sense in the world, and none at all, both at the same time. But as the cane hovered in midair and the shadow neared, she knew what must be done.

She turned and grabbed hold of the back of the bench, bending over, presenting her bottom to the Master. A hot hand pushed her skirt up to her waist, exposing her ass to the sun. She was strong enough, she'd see, all she had to do was just hold on—

The first smack was an unexpected flash of pain. She didn't know what she'd thought it would feel like—she hadn't thought at all—but she didn't know how bad it would sting. It hurt, it really hurt, there was so much pain she didn't know what to do with it, where all of it should go, and before she could figure it out—

The second stroke one sent her up on her toes, hissing, fingers clawed into the back of the bench as she choked back more tears. Nerves just on the edge of quieting stung her, furious with her for letting them get smacked not once but twice—

And then the third blow landed.

She cried out, unable to help herself.

There was the sound of running on gravel and the cane dropped and she pushed her skirt back down, facing to see who had come to her rescue.

It was Richard. With the sunlight behind him, he looked like a knight in shining armor, and she felt ashamed about the painful streaks across her ass.

"I'm okay," she said, trying to allay him.

"The market's crashed in Paris. If I'm not there in person," he began, the second he saw her.

He kept talking as she tried to parse his words, blood rushing in her ears. He hadn't heard her cry out and come running—he hadn't come out to rescue her. He'd come out to tell her he had to leave, again. She was so dumbfounded by this that she blurted out, "You can't go."

He blinked and pulled back as though she'd slapped him. "I have to. The driver's on the way."

"No." Her hands found the top button on her shirt-dress and undid it. "I'm your wife." Her hands sank to the second button, the third. "I need a baby, Richard. This house—it's too much for me, all alone."

"I swear, the second I get back, we'll make one—we'll make twins, if we have to." He was trying to make jokes, now that he realized how deadly serious she'd become.

"I want you now, Richard. I need you now. I need you to put me first." She reached the last of the buttons and let the shirt dress fall to the ground. If the sun backlighting him turned him into a knight, then all of it on her exposed skin now turned her into a glowing angel. She could see the indecision on his face, how he fought with himself, the outline of his cock growing against his dress pants.

"Pet, I can't. I barely have time to pack and print my tickets." He crossed the space to her though anyhow, grabbing her to him roughly, his hands groping her ass where it still burned from the cane. "It's only three days. I promise I'll fuck you the moment I return."

She didn't say anything, she didn't want to grant him permission, or even tell him good-bye. He let go of her and, sensing her change, stalked off, to convince himself he was doing the right thing no doubt. She waited until he was gone, picked her dress back up to put it on, and found Arthur on her way inside the house.

"Please call Mr. Sanderson and see when he'll be available next."

"Of course, Ma'am."

THE CANING HURT her for the rest of the day. Every time she sat she remembered it, and there was no way to avoid sitting. Instead of reminding her how she'd been strong and what she'd survived, the pain only echoed Richard's betrayal. Off again. For 'business'. Of course.

Daphne wandered down into his study, to where he'd set up his computer. She would order pregnancy tests, in bulk. Spending his money vengefully was the only thing she could do to hurt him.

The second she was pregnant, she'd be free. And nine months later when she was holding a baby—she would get a divorce. Keep the house, and keep the child, and that would be that.

She shook the mouse and the screen blinked to life. She was searching for the most expensive shipping option when a small window popped up.

Beccababy93: *You there?*

The cursor fluttered in time with her heartbeat.

Call me?

Can't, Daphne typed back, slowly. *Wife.*

She ruins everything.

Daphne puckered her lips, looking at the screen, trying to decide what precisely to do next. A few short days ago she would have closed the screen and just stepped away. But now—like a child who couldn't stop playing with fire, she knew she wanted their conversation to go on. *Not everything. She gives excellent blow-jobs.*

You said mine were better! Low. Daphne squinted at the screen. She couldn't push too hard—but what would look better in divorce court than a transcript of some woman recounting memories of her time with Richard?

I did? She hit return. It was the kind of imperious thing Richard would say. *Remind me which one? In particular. Use details.*

A long pause, in which Daphne feared she'd overplayed her hand.

Paris? Or London?

Both, Daphne typed, and then sat back.

WHAT FOLLOWED WERE FAIRLY pedestrian narratives. Funny stories about getting caught in the rain, hiding from a gendarme in a park, fate throwing them together—or throwing her at his cock. Daphne watched the words scroll across the screen and it felt like someone else was reading them, not her. She said nothing, which only encouraged the other woman to go to greater lengths, perhaps fearing she was losing her *dearest Richard* to the warm arms of his wife. Daphne breathed in and out dispassionately as the woman finished up, and cut and paste everything into a separate screen to print it off for later.

Is everything okay? BeccaBaby93 had nervously asked in 'Richard's' absence.

Leave her hanging? Write things out of spite? Tell her the truth? Pretend 'Richard' was getting called away?

The moment hovered, stretching out uncomfortably long, and then the temperature in the room jumped up around Daphne like someone had turned on a nearby oven. She waved her hands around herself—the ghost was near, not tangible yet, but close by.

Everything's fine. Keys on the keyboard in front of her moved, soundlessly, and the letters the ghost was typing appeared.

You were so quiet, Becca typed back quickly.

My hands were too busy to type.

Daphne straightened and turned. Had he been reading over her shoulder? Had Becca's pathetic retelling of a blowjob turned him on? She flushed with anger and shame—she couldn't be losing out to Becca with the Master, too.

Tell me what you're going to do to me when you see me next, Becca prompted.

Daphne rolled her eyes.

Do you really want to know? the ghost typed back.

Yes.

Are you sure? the ghost teased, after just the perfect amount of time passed. Daphne could imagine Becca wriggling in her seat on the far end of the line, a worm caught on a hook.

Yes! Tell me!

You want to see into the filthy blackness of my heart?

You know I love it when you talk dirty. Daphne almost felt bad for the girl then, trying desperately to keep her husband—a man who clearly played with women like dice—interested in her. And then Becca typed in some emoticon, a smiley face with large innocently blinking eyes and Daphne wanted to swat the monitor to the ground. *I hope the Master gives you what you deserve,* Daphne thought, and pushed back from the keyboard.

The ghost took this for the permission that it was, and words began to flood the screen.

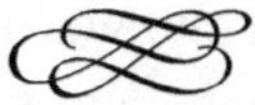

CHAPTER 12

*W*hat if I did more than talk?

What if I really were dirty?

What if there were things about me that I could never change? Things I've never dared to show you? Things I've been dying to share?

Daphne swallowed and leaned forward to read.

I just bought a new estate. Imagine my surprise when I was unpacking our first night and found a hidden door.

What was behind it? Becca asked.

Shhh. I'll tell this story my own way, at my own pace.

Another pregnant pause.

Just for you.

I OPENED up the door and walked down its stairs with a flashlight. There were cobwebs and dust, and I knew that no one had been down there for a very, very long time.

And when I got to the bottom of the stair I looked around—there were things there. Strange pieces of furniture, wood and metal, bound with dark leather. I walked among them and stroked my hand along their smooth *curves and knew what they were for and felt...at peace. As though, despite the entire house being mine, and having owned houses before this one, that I had at last truly come home.*

Daphne crept to the end of her chair, imagining Becca mirroring her on the far side.

Do you want to know what I would do to you there? If you were here? If my troublesome wife weren't in the way?

Daphne pursed her lips at the word troublesome. No doubt that was how Richard thought of her, and yet.

Yes, Becca typed and the ghost continued.

I would blindfold you first. Then I would take your hand and pull you to the stairway I'd found and take you down the stairs, one by one by one. You would have to trust me with the blindfold on. You'd have no choice.

I could always take the blindfold off, Becca typed.

But you wouldn't. If you take it off, the story would be over, wouldn't it? And you don't want it to end yet, do you?

The cursor blinked beside the question mark for a long while. *No. Good.*

Another pause, as if 'Richard' were deciding whether or not to go on. Daphne knew her husband was as straight as an arrow, and he'd never put a hand on her, during sex or otherwise. She wondered if his relationship with this Becca were different...or if Becca was stunned by the slightly dangerous turn this story was taking and if, wherever it was that she was typing from now, she were turned on.

I lead you down into the basement—no, not a basement, that's not the right word for it, though that's what it is. It's a dungeon. And it's full of things that haven't been used in years...and I'm desperate for a chance to use them.

There's a table. Waist height. I take you over to it and push you down on it, and you can feel its chill against the weight of your breasts as I tie your arms.

You feel my hand against your back, stroking the softness of the skin I'm about to mar, and you flinch, not knowing what will happen, only that you're chained and you can't do anything to protect yourself against what's coming next—

I swat you, with a tease, open handed. The sound of it echoes in the small room, the crisp sound of flesh on flesh. You shiver and whimper, a little scared, but more turned on.

Shall I spank you again, dearest?

Daphne swallowed. The ghost was playing with Becca—and with her.

Yes. Becca's response was tentative, but Daphne's wasn't. Daphne let her knees slide apart, and started slowly moving her hand up her thigh.

A torrent of words filled the screen. The ghost explained in intricate, daring, detail what would happen to the kind of girls who left themselves blindfolded in strange houses at night. Whatever fear or shame Daphne might have had fell by the wayside as she read each delicious line—knowing he was writing it for her. Becca's presence was merely an afterthought—but knowing that she was waiting on the far end, just as eager as she was for the next word, was a strange turn on. It shouldn't have been, but it was. Daphne's fingers were circling her clit through her underwear, in turns rough and soft, and her breathing was coming out in shallow pants and she was holding onto the chair with her freehand because she might fall over if she let go— she was so close, her toes were pointed, her calves tight, as she imagined herself tied to the table, as the Master's cock started to slide in and out—she bit back a moan and rubbed herself harder.

Words flared on Becca's side. *Husband home! GTG!*

There was an excruciating pause where Daphne kept her heat up, willing the ghost to go on with his story —

We HAVE to do this again, Becca typed, before logging off.

"Please," Daphne begged in real life. "Tell me the end."

The sensation of heat, outside and within, began to fade.

"No—I'm so close—please." But the screen went black, and Daphne sagged back against the chair, sitting in a pool of her own desires and frustration.

. . .

DAPHNE SPENT the rest of the evening before dinner looking for the door. She had no doubt that it existed—the ghost described it too perfectly for that. But how to get there from here? That was the question. She began her inquiries on the upper wing of the other floor.

She traced her hand around floorboards, underneath the massive bed left behind, and against the back walls of closets, knocking, listening for hollow points.

The house was so complicated and so old though—there could be twenty hidden passageways—the whole thing could be like an episode of Scooby Doo, and she wouldn't know until she tripped into the right wall sconce.

During all of her searches, she knew the ghost was near. Watching her. Feeding off her hope and her frustration, probably laughing to himself at her grasping blindly at anything that could get her back to that table and his cock.

"This is epically unfair," she complained aloud, after searching the last room. She thought she heard him chuckle from beside her—and then Arthur ring for dinner.

"ARTHUR," she asked by the third course, "Do you know of any secret passageways? Or rooms?"

Arthur seemed taken aback by the question. "No, Ma'am. Have you found one?"

"Oh, no." She let her voice drift off. "I was just thinking. A big house like this has to have two or three."

"They used to put them in on purpose in the old days, so that you wouldn't have to see the servants scurrying about."

"Really?"

"Well, and to hide treasures. In the old days, it was also hard to count on banks."

Daphne grinned at the old man with affection. "I think you're pulling my leg."

"Scout's honor, Ma'am," he said, grinning back, and picking up her plate. "I called Mr. Sanderson. He'll come by after work tomorrow. Seemed very pleased to get the chance to help us with the dresser."

"And I'll be pleased to finally have it moved. Thank you Arthur."

"You're welcome. Anything else?"

"Nothing at all."

"See you for breakfast then, Ma'am," Arthur said, and left with a bow.

DAPHNE SAT at the table a while longer, listening to Arthur and Mrs. Dudley leave. The Master had been taunting her all day, and now it was his turn to be taunted, just a little bit. He couldn't know what it was that she'd do, not one hundred percent—he could only hope that she'd do it.

Daphne took herself on a tour of the house, intoxicated by the idea of what would happen if she let it, trying to stretch the anticipation out. Feeling regal, she looked around each room with a future eye— how new paintings would be commissioned and hung, new rugs rolled out, vast arrangements of flowers, the statues displayed like the works of art they were, always keeping a feel for the pulse of the house's original grandeur and majesty. She would restore it to its glory days, and it would love her for it, and it would love her baby.

She made her way up to where her nursery would be and imagined a crib with a lazy mobile circling above it—and then went into the green room, where she'd left the picture of the horse-girl. Daphne stared down at it. Had she been raised her whole life here? How lucky she had been, and how profoundly sad her ending.

Just as Daphne lowered the photo she thought she saw a figure behind the girl in it. She blinked and squinted. Had it been there before? Was it there now? She wavered, trying to bring things into focus again, and then realized it was time to stop fighting what she wanted.

In less than twenty glorious feet she was back in her bedroom again.

· · ·

DAPHNE UNDRESSED CARELESSLY, dropping her skirt and shirt to the floor, leaving only her underwear and bra on. Then she rummaged in her closet until she found a scarf. It was sheer, but if she tied it twice, it would do.

Sitting on the edge of the bed, she lassoed it and knotted it behind her so that it covered her eyes. And then deliberately she swung both her legs up and lay atop her mattress, arms crossed on her chest as if she were dead.

The only question was how long would he make her wait? They'd been teasing each other since this afternoon, first his making her search, and then her taking her time, each pretending that they were fighting ending up right here…and yet here she was.

So where was he? Daphne licked her lips, a little nervous—and then felt a hot hand on her arm.

Hands trailed slowly over her body, enveloping her in his heat for long enough that she felt chilled when they were gone. She wished he were a blanket, that she could pull him over him and feel safe in him—but that wasn't their kind of relationship. She had safe with Richard, and what had it gotten her? Taken for granted and cheated on.

Better yet that she be with someone dangerous, someone who kept her on her toes. Someone that she couldn't let her guard down around so that when she finally gave in it felt so much sweeter.

The hands finally paused over her hands, taking them up, pulling her to seated, then to standing as she let them.

Her heart started beating in her throat. This was really happening. The things she'd seen him threaten Becca with were promises for her. There would be a door, a table, chains, and—she paused in exhilarating fear and felt him near behind her, prodding her forward with his erection—and let out a gasp, and thought she could feel-hear the ghost rumble, like distant thunder.

He spun her in several directions, and then moved to lead her, just as he'd typed, through a door and down a stair. She followed, bare feet on cold stone, down and down, her clit thudding between her legs with each step, her hips aching, need unresolved since this afternoon sparking into something sharper and more hungry.

The ghost paused and she paused, and she was dying to take off her blindfold and look around. But then where would she be? And he might not deign to fuck her after that. He was in control—always had been. And she…she needed to be fucked. In such a brutal, primal way.

The ghost pulled her forward again, until she felt something cold and curved across her hips. It gave a little, which was good, because the ghost grabbed a hand into her hair and brought her bending over it. Cushioned leather? She had just long enough to make a guess, before her hands were pulled down—and chains attached them to her ankles.

Daphne fought after this. She wondered why she was fighting—why she hadn't fought seconds earlier when she could have gotten away, and why it was important that she was fighting now, when she absolutely could not. Was she fighting for herself, or for him, or just to fight? Just to be forced to admit that she couldn't get free, that she'd invited this upon her own fool self? Or because she needed to make sure the chains were tight, to show herself that in his twisted way he wanted her, needed her, so much so that he made sure she couldn't run?

The chains rattled and she knew no one would hear them or her, panting awkwardly, blood rushing to her head, feeling dizzy and out of control before he'd even begun, knowing that her ass was stuck up in the air. And when she was done panicking, when the exhilaration of being trapped had begun to ever so slightly curdle with a hint of fear, he started.

His hands were hot again, on her, pawing her back roughly, massaging the muscles that her awkward position pulled. He took hold of her ass and thighs like she were a piece of meat, kneading her with strong fingers, feeling the tension inside her ass and thighs, the tension on her that this position caused.

Daphne yanked on the chains again, and then she stilled. The only sound in the room was the sound of her panting breath, the cushion caught up in her stomach and under her ribs so she couldn't fully breathe.

"What would you say to me if you could?" she whispered.

The hands grasping her paused, as if in thought. And then he took a step towards her and she could feel the heat of his erection against the cleft of her ass.

And that, she supposed, nearly upside down and lost and confused was all he really needed to say.

CHAPTER 13

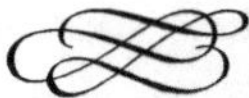

He reached between them and pushed his cock down so that it slid between her legs, and his head rubbed up against her clit. Behind her his thighs lined up with hers and he leaned over her, covering her with his heat, then scratched fingers down her back while pulsing himself against her, chaste by only the most technical definition of the word. It was like he was trying to merge with her, become one with her, envelope her inside him.

And then it was his turn to be inside her. He repositioned himself, and she wasn't fully wet, but he slid in anyway, all hot and hard. She grunted gutturally at being entered like that, and then it was like a faucet turned on inside of her, she was a fountain, she felt it covering him and then running down the insides of her thighs.

What followed wasn't sex. Not compared to any kind of sex she'd ever had before. She didn't know what it was—she only knew that he wanted her and he'd chained her up and he was going to fuck her until she couldn't take it anymore and then possibly beyond. Her hair was dragging on the ground and all she could feel was the stone with her toes, her ankles with her hands, the bar beneath her hips and his cock ramming into her, bruising her against the bar, over and over.

All this time he'd always helped her come—made her come—but she'd never once managed to satisfy him. The time in the bathroom that Richard had interrupted hardly counted—maybe this was what he needed to get off, to be totally, utterly, in control.

At the thought of her finally taming him, even if it took this—she spread her legs wider to withstand his assault. He made a sound at this, or she thought he did, and then she started shouting with each of his thrusts. Animal sounds—lost sounds—because she knew no one would hear—and if no one could save her now, neither could they condemn.

"Fuck me," she shouted out, an exclamation—but he took it as a command. The friction between them, his heat sliding in and out, the fact that she was trapped here and couldn't get away—she wanted to get her hands free, desperately, she needed to rub her clit, she wanted her pussy to wind around him and make him hers—but she wanted him to come more, and harder, than he ever had before in his life—or the next. "Fuck me, fuck me, fuck me," she cried, her voice rising in a whine.

Hands grabbed her hips roughly, riding himself inside her in time with her words.

"Don't ever stop—just keep fucking me—" her body vibrated with the words, with him ramming into her, her pussy being filled again and again.

His hands left her, and they must have grabbed hold of the bar she was slung across because she felt the whole thing rattle as he yanked back, making her whole body sway, limp as a rag doll.

"Fuck, fuck, fuck," she whispered, her pussy quivering on the edge even without her clit, and behind her the ghost shuddered, bodily, three final times, hauling her back across the beam she lay on, to finish spearing her with his hot cock. She imagined she could feel his cum inside her, blazing a hot molten trail, before sliding out again.

She couldn't breathe. She just lay there, chained, and whimpered. She wasn't angry or sad—there was no room for thoughts anymore inside her head. Heat pulled away from her, left her standing and cold, wetness flowing between her thighs, and she had a dizzy thought that he might leave her like this and never let her go—but it didn't matter. Nothing mattered right now, not anymore.

The chains holding her wrist to ankle fell free and hands almost helped her to standing before she fell through them, on weak legs, to the ground with a thump.

Warmth enveloped her again, more gently now, holding her from behind, an arm underneath her gravity swollen breasts and bar-bruised waist. He rocked her, the ghost, slowly, as though she were a child, and from some well deep inside she started crying. Honest, frustrated tears—crying for everything she'd lost with Richard, all the time and all the hope, every time she'd been ignorant and dumb and played a fool. It was like the Master's cock were a stick and it'd stirred up the very bottom of a very deep pond inside her, one that would never be all the way clear again. Daphne knew she'd never manage to be as innocent as she once had been. It was like growing up, and it felt awful.

She curled forward, sobbing, and the Master held her, stroking back her hair from her face, his heat the only solace she had in the darkness. It wouldn't matter how long she cried, or how hard, or how ugly she'd be afterwards—she wasn't going to scare him away. The knowledge of that was her only tow-line back to sanity from the raw and unbound place she'd been.

When she could breathe again, she felt his fingers on her face, slipping underneath her blindfold, touching the trails of her tears. And then that same hand lowered down between her sprawled open legs and touched her softly there and she gasped.

She would have thought any fire there had been entirely quenched by her crying, but no—her tears had only washed everything clean. She was in a place beyond trust or fear, a land of pure openness, and she moaned with his next touch.

She felt him rumble behind her, pleased with her release—pleased to be retaking control again. He didn't need the chains and he didn't need the bar, he just pulled her back into his arms. One hand cradled a breast and rolled her nipple between finger and thumb and the other rubbed at her clit.

She crossed her arms over his, holding herself tighter to him, pinching her other nipple, feeling the curve of his body behind hers, the heat where his stomach met her back. His fingers played inside her now, brought out her wetness and circled her with it, teasing at her most electric spot, before darting back inside, taunting her, listening to her gasp.

He played her and she let him. She gave into it as she'd never given into anything before. She relaxed and let him have utter, utter, control, even moreso than she had while she'd been chained. She willed herself into the experience and then released any hopes she had, any desires, any needs, as she felt his fingers pinch and pull and fill her up. She heard her own voice as from a great distance, and it was like he'd turned her into an instrument, one only he could play. She responded to everything he did, moaning, gasps, panting, whines, muttered prayers to don't stop, never stop again—

And then she was there, closer to coming that she'd ever been aware of before, not a sharp bright edge to fall over but a wall of delicious light to push through, radiating out from her over her entire body, from fingertip to fingertip, from toe to head—

And then she hit the hardest orgasm she'd ever had in her life on the other side. Her body roiled like she'd been flung on rocks, curved over and pulled tight, muscles taut and then utterly released, again and again. She was shouting, she heard herself shouting, she knew she was shouting, and then she relaxed into a moan, falling through, falling down until she remembered where she was, on the ground in a secret dungeon being held by a particularly talented ghost.

And at last she laughed. Her voice was strange and harsh from all the other sounds she'd made tonight, but the joy was genuine and it burbled up from inside her, a secret place that she never knew she had and she thought she might never find again. The ghost—the Master, her Master, her beloved Master, stood himself and then carefully helped her to stand. Then he pulled her up stairs, made sure she was steady, and led her through her own house until making her stop on what she knew was tile and drew her a hot bath.

Daphne stepped into the tub gingerly, and felt the steam of the water replace the heat of his hands, and reached up for the blindfold to tug it down. She was alone, except for the swirl of steam where she thought he had just been.

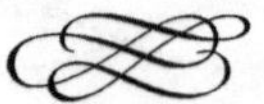

CHAPTER 14

"M a'am?"

Daphne woke to Arthur's polite knocking at her door in the morning.

"Did I oversleep?"

"You did, Ma'am," Arthur said, through the door.

"I'm so sorry." She scrabbled for her phone with one hand. No signal, but it'd been an excellent alarm clock—up until she'd forgotten to set it.

"It's all right Ma'am—I just wanted to see if you were well."

"I am, Arthur. Just a little too much wine after you left last night was all." And…other things. Had everything really happened? Or had it all just been one elaborate dream?

"Shall we be seeing you for lunch in about an hour then, Ma'am?"

"That'd be perfect, Arthur."

With him away from her door, she could think.

What proof did she have that last night had even happened? She kicked off her sheets and found out—her arms and legs were stiff, and her pussy and hips were sore.

God. It had been real. All the magical oddity of it. She'd never been like that before, and it'd never felt so good for her—she could still remember the sensation of that orgasm, like she'd been falling through time and space—her hands wound in the sheets just thinking of it.

Could it be like that here, every night?

If it was, would she survive it?

She looked around the room, as though the Master might be looking in and then laughed at herself. Richard's escapades—whoever he was doing, wherever he was—had nothing on her.

DAPHNE TOOK ANOTHER SHOWER, at the end of which she only felt like she'd worked out hard the day before. She carefully dried her hair and put on just enough make-up to look 'natural', whatever that was for someone who was getting regularly fucked by a ghost.

She took a seat at the end of the table, as Arthur brought her lunch.

"You look lovely, Ma'am."

"Thank you."

"You're positively glowing," he went on.

"Must be all the beauty rest," she said distractedly, pulling her chair in.

DAPHNE SPENT most of lunch toying with it. After last night…what did she owe the Master? She couldn't fall in love with him—he wasn't really there. But he made her feel, so intensely—was he just using her? Was she just using him? Why did she have to think about it so much now?

The last, she knew the answer to, at least, if she were honest with herself. There was only one reason she'd asked Luke to come over and it had nothing to do with moving the dresser. After last night she felt the owed the Master if not monogamy, then an explanation.

"Not hungry, Ma'am?" Arthur inquired, after a polite time had passed.

"Not really. A little nauseous is all."

"Do you need a doctor? We could go into town —"

"Oh, no, that's all right—" She bit the inside of her lip. "I'm fine now. Just come and get me when Mr. Sanderson arrives, please."

"Of course, Ma'am."

Leaving Arthur behind with dishes, she slunk out into the hall—and then into the library, where the Master's portrait was staring down. She stood in the middle of the room and knew he was here, even if he wasn't touching her.

"Please don't be mad."

If last night was him in a good mood, she didn't think her body could stand it if she made him angry.

"You do understand what I want here, don't you?" she asked him, and swallowed. "It's not that I don't want to stay here—because I do. You know I do. I want to be with you. But—I also want a child—and you can't give me that. Please don't be mad."

Daphne got the sensation of electricity around her, like she was standing on a hill in the middle of a thunderstorm. She turned around to look over her shoulders, feeling like he might be standing there. Then she shook herself and took a strong stance.

"I'm not asking for forgiveness—or permission. I'm just asking you to understand."

Before lightning could strike her or the portrait come to life, she heard the melodious chimes of the doorbell being rung from the back door, and she raced to pretend she'd been waiting upstairs this whole time.

Daphne heard Arthur let Luke in. "So good of you to come, Mr. Sanderson."

"It's fine, I was in the neighborhood this morning."

She slowed and descended the final few stairs with decorum and a smile. "Luke. Thanks for coming," she said, overly innocent.

He looked up at her and smirked a little. He hadn't forgotten their rendezvous and she felt a current pass between them, same as it had when she'd been framed by her window and he'd eagerly watched.

"You're welcome," he said, equally innocent. "So where's this dresser?" he said and looked around, arms flexed.

WITH LUKE'S help they were able to move the dresser into its final position, and a number of other small items of furniture, including some of the statues.

He refused to let her help, worried that she'd hurt herself or get dirty in turns, and instead used every opportunity he had to show himself off to her, like this was some sort of audition, which, Daphne realized, it sort of was. She couldn't feel the Master's disapproving looming anymore, and hoped that he'd gotten over his anger from this morning as Luke moved the last piece of carved wood.

"Are you sure that's not a door stopper?"

"I think it's supposed to be modern." She tilted her head. "But now that you mention it—I wouldn't place bets." She laughed and he laughed, and Arthur returned.

"More tea?" he offered.

"No, thank you," Luke said, straightening up. "I'm done for the day. It's time to go home," he said, looking at her, and she flushed.

A man had his pride. It was her turn.

"I do have a question about the stable, after all. Since you're here—can I show you?" she asked. She felt like the words were rushing out of her mouth, too fast.

He leaned against the wall behind him and squinted his eyes knowingly at her, taking all of her in. "Of course."

CHAPTER 15

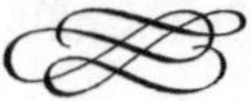

Daphne walked outside reluctantly. It wasn't that she didn't want this, it was just that she felt like it was going to be up to her to proposition him. It was one thing in the window, separated by space and glass—this was different. It was real.

Someone could get hurt.

Luke followed her, half a step behind, silent. She wished he would talk, but then what? What if he said the wrong thing? Silence was better, even if it gave her too much space to think.

Her heart started beating doubletime as the outline of the stable emerged beyond a copse of trees. It was noon, the sun was beating down, the shade inside would feel so cool—especially if she were naked. She glanced over at him and saw him watching her, that same even gaze he'd used all day, weighing, measuring. She felt hotter than she had any right to be, and something inside her shivered at the thought of touching his skin, and felt the parts of her that she wanted him to be in lightly squeeze. She had no right to be ready for sex again this soon, not after last night. But instead of satisfying her, the Master's cock had only made her aware of how often she was starving.

They reached the stable and stepped inside. It smelled musty and old but not bad, and scattered piles of hay were dry.

"Have you seen the old workshop yet?"

Daphne shook her head.

"It's probably not safe to go up there," he said, then grinned. "So we definitely should. Come on." He jerked his chin at a narrow stair and started taking steps up two at a time.

Daphne followed him. This wasn't how she had planned things—if she could have been said to have planned them at all.

"It's the old man's workspace—where he created all that 'art' inside your house." Luke said the word mockingly. "But maybe he just needed an excuse to get out of his house. It's not like they had TVs out here back then. Who can say."

Daphne stepped up behind him and looked around. There were shelves of tools, neat and orderly, rows of metal things hanging against the walls, just where the Master had left them. Like he would come back at any time.

And there were half formed carved blocks here. More of the statuary, similar to what was inside, only still straining to get out. Figures of angels and demons, struggling not only with one another, but with the wood they were left trapped in, without the Master's freeing hand. Daphne stroked a finger in the dust over the nearest statue, tracing the curve of an angel's wing.

"I'd seen this place before—but I'd never seen any of the finished ones before today."

"You'd never been inside of the house?" Daphne looked over at him.

"No."

"Why not?"

He snorted and grinned ruefully. "No one ever invited me in." He looked at her meaningfully, and then took a stronger stance, separating his legs like he was a drill instructor.

"So just what did you want done out here?" He looked directly at her and she swallowed.

"Are you going to make me ask for it?"

His eyebrow quirked, and his lips subtly pursed. "I'm afraid I am going to need to hear it out loud, yes. I'm not in the habit of assuming I can fuck my employers—or letting them fuck with me."

That set her off her game. "Does this happen often enough you need a policy?"

"You're not the first rich lady to think she owns me," he said, his eyes studying her hard. Daphne was suddenly disappointed in herself for being so trite, and her shoulders sagged, which he noted and shook his head in admonishment. "You are, however, the first to fuck me through a window. Which I admit greatly brightened my day." He took a step closer to her and her breath caught in her throat. She could smell the sweat of his day, the green grass he'd been cutting earlier hovering around him like an earthy perfume.

"You do want this, don't you?" he asked her, eyes dark.

"Yes, please, yes."

His full lips parted into a smile. "Good."

THERE WAS A TANGLE OF CLOTHING. He pulled her shirt up over her head, exposing her skin for his hands and his mouth found hers as she reached for his shirt, pulling it out of his jeans. He was taller than she was, as tall as Richard, and it was easy to rock with his kisses, to let his tongue into her mouth and taste the eagerness to have her there.

She ran her hands down his smooth chest and felt the muscles bunch as she did so, him shuddering like a stallion, knowing his turn—their turn—was about to come.

He picked her up easily and dropped her into a nearby pile of hay. It poked and scratched at her until she squirmed to smooth it and then his mouth found her ear, her collarbone, and the musky weight of his body was so close. She gasped a sigh for him and a rough hand reached under her bra to feel her breast, then pull it up, showing more of her to him, his tan skin against hers so pale and white. His afternoon old beard grazed her on his way down, following his trail of kisses down to where his mouth took in her nipple and sucked at it, sending a bolt of electricity straight between her thighs. He moved from one breast to the next, kissing, touching, the roughness of his beard, the softness of his tongue, until his hands found the edge of her skirt and folded it up just like her bra and pulled her panties down.

Being kissed on her clit by a stranger was just like being kissed on the mouth by one, surprising, strange, unexpected yet comfortable. She looked down at him, seeing his dark hair bob between her open thighs, and she moaned as his tongue traced up her folds, lapping at her hidden spots.

"Oh—oh yes." She ran her fingers across his scalp and arched to claw them up his back before relenting to the sensation of his tongue, and he purred every time she groaned, her hips beginning to twitch in his wake.

Luke pulled himself up and kicked off his shoes and shoved down his pants—but not before retrieving something from his pocket. She heard the sound of the wrapper, but it took her a moment to place what it was, as she saw him reaching for his hard cock.

"No—don't." She pushed his hands away, and he eyed her warily.

"Why not?"

"Because." And here was the part where she would sound crazy. "I don't want you to use one. I want to have a baby."

"No way," he said, leveraging himself further back.

"No—really. My husband—we're trying, but it's not working out, and—he'll never know. I'll never tell him. I'm rich, you said it yourself —but this is the one thing I can't buy."

"There's ways…" he said, shaking his head.

"They take so long. And they're not this fun." She took her hand away from him and put it on his shoulder. "Please."

His hand holding the condom wavered. And then slowly, ever so slowly, he set it down. Sensing he'd decided, she wordlessly leaned up and took her bra off, and then lay back.

He'd been taking his time before, but he took even longer now. He pulled his jeans all the way off, and then lowered himself back down beside her, his body aligned with hers, and pulled her to him, onto her side and hip, pulling her leg over his side. And when he entered her he watched her face like he was trying to memorize it.

He didn't fuck her—instead he rocked with her, kissing her, holding her close, and Daphne thought if there really was a way to make sure you had a child, this was it. She bowed her head in and let him hold her, breathing him in, hoping this moment would take. She didn't want to come—would that be a betrayal? To who? Was there anything left to betray?—but she felt the friction building inside of her, his gentleness stoking the embers of her fire. She started panting in his ear and she could tell he was holding himself back, waiting for her to release first—her hands held onto his shoulders and she bit her lips instead of crying out because it was like it didn't count if she could keep the sound inside.

He felt her though, her pussy squeezing him tight, and his hands cupped her ass, bringing her closer—she felt him thrust into her and then gasp out as he came, his hips spasming into hers before slickly parting, and they were two naked strangers holding one another again.

"Thank you," Daphne breathed out, trying to keep her legs closed. *Please work. Please, please.*

"You're welcome," he said. The emotions on his face were hard to read, and he seemed unsure. Which was a good thing, wasn't it? She didn't want a child with someone who always thought they knew what was right, like Richard did.

"You do this sort of thing a lot?" she asked, not sure if she really wanted the answer.

"You're not my first rodeo. But the baby thing—that's new," he said, shaking his head lightly.

"I'm sorry. I so appreciate it—this—" she touched his chest carefully. Despite what they'd just shared, there was a gulf growing between them now. "My husband is gone a lot."

His brow furrowed. "I'm not sure if I should say I'm sorry to hear that or not."

"Me either. But thank you. I mean it."

His eyes studied hers a moment more, and then he reached up to stroke her hair back from her forehead. "You'd probably better get back now, before Arthur gets worried."

She nodded. She wanted to keep his cum inside her—and more than that, keep him there—but she stood nonetheless. He followed her up, pulling her skirt down for her and dusting the hay off. She pulled her underwear up demurely and tugged her bra back on while he reassembled himself not that far away.

They descended the stairs, looking much the same as they had when they'd gone up, only now a little sweatier, with secret smiles.

"When will you know if it takes?" Luke asked.

"Soon, I hope. A few days."

He nodded, licking his lips. "What if it doesn't?"

"Then…" she looked at the ground, afraid to ask for what she wanted again.

"Your husband is gone a lot, isn't he?" Luke said.

"He is." Relief blossomed inside of her, right beside hope.

"So then…we'll see."

She gave him a tentative smile. "We will." She danced backwards, like one of the high spirited horses that used to stay here, sending a long forgotten riding crop spinning away from one foot. It caught her eye and she chased after it, picking it up, all while Luke watched.

"What's that?" he asked her, still looking at her like she was something strange—but also lovely.

Her eyes cast on the crop's braided sheath and dusty leather end, then she smiled at him. "It's a souvenir," she said, and practically skipped home.

CHAPTER 16

$\mathcal{A}$rthur wasn't waiting for her when she got back, which was perfect. She raced upstairs to her bedroom and closed the door. Maybe, just maybe—she threw herself onto her bed and cupped one hand to her belly.

Did the Master know what she'd done? Would he forgive her? She raised the other hand with the whip in it—she thought she knew how to make him.

"Ma'am?"

Arthur knocked on her door, rousing her from a light nap.

"Yes?" Sleeping was good, it gave her a reason for disarray, other than her interlude in the barn. She still smelled a little like dust and sweat, and even though she ought to, she didn't want to wash it off.

"Dinner's going to be a little late. The milk's gone bad, and I need to go into town to get more for Mrs. Dudley."

"That's okay—I can eat a sandwich, honestly," Daphne got out of bed and crossed the room to the door. "Unless—Arthur—I want to go into town with you."

"Really, Ma'am? There's not much to it."

"No, I want to. Please. Give me five minutes, and I can meet you by the front door."

"All right."

She changed clothing quickly, then went into the bathroom to brush out her hair and spritz on perfume. It wasn't like she'd know anyone in the town, and yet she felt she must meet a minimum standard for decorum. As the mistress of a house this grand—if anyone still remembered it was here—she felt presentability was expected of her.

Returning to her room, she smoothed the sheets, and placed the riding crop squarely in the center of the bed. An offering for her dark god, herself the future lamb.

Pleased with this, she trotted down the stairs and found Arthur waiting. He bowed, and escorted her into his car.

The driveway wound and curved and she felt an almost physical pang as they passed through the final gate, leaving the house's land behind.

"How many grocery stores are there in town?"

"Just one. It's more of a market. That's why we have to go now, they close after six."

"Oh." Daphne chewed on her lower lip. "What about other stores?"

"There's a feed and tack store, a gas station, a hardware store, a few antique stores, and one small diner. And that's about it, I'm afraid." Arthur sounded genuinely apologetic. "People come here to leave the hustle and bustle of the city behind. That's why it's such a good place to raise children. It's so safe out here."

Daphne nodded deeply. There was another reason she hadn't showered after sleeping with Luke today. She didn't want to wash his cum away, not when she was praying so hard it would take.

Arthur parked outside the market. It was hardly bigger than her house's library. "I'll just be a moment. Or, would you like to come inside?"

The market was on the 'main' street, apparently along with every other storefront Arthur had named for her. "No—I'm going to go look in some windows."

"All right, Ma'am. I'll be back in a little bit." He grinned at her. "Don't worry, I won't leave without you."

DAPHNE HOPPED out of the car and walked down the street. There were a few people out, and she heard the susurration of cars zipping past on the road, off to more interesting places to be. She peeked in the windows of the hardware store and the diner, and then walked over to the nearest antique store. There were shelves and shelves of knick-knacks, carefully arranged and gathering dust. She opened the door and a bell chimed over head as she stepped inside.

"Hi, can I help you?" a woman asked, her voice preceding her.

Daphne looked up and was surprised to see a small blonde woman her own age. She'd assumed everyone in town was as ancient as Arthur—even if Luke had already proven her wrong.

"Oh, I'm just looking," Daphne said.

"Passing through?" the woman guessed.

"No—I just moved here last week."

"Really? A new neighbor! Did you buy the place up on Westridge?"

"No—the house around the bend—" Daphne was sure the house had a name, but she didn't know what it was yet.

The woman's eyes widened in excitement. "With the long driveway and the stable out back? I hadn't heard that it sold! About time!"

"You know about it?"

"Of course! My aunt used to work there!"

It was Daphne's turn to brighten. "That's amazing—can I meet her? I'd love to know the place's history."

The woman made an apologetic face. "We can ask her, but it's hard to say how helpful she'd be. She's at a nursing home near the coast, she has Alzheimer's."

Daphne put a hand to her chest. "Oh, I'm so sorry."

"Don't be, you couldn't have known," the blonde shook her head and smiled. "Did the prior owners empty it out?"

"What?"

"A lot of big estates, the families just get overwhelmed—or the places are so big, things just get lost, things that used to have meaning just go and get left behind." She pointed to their surroundings. "Sorry —professional curiosity."

Daphne snorted. "I think it's a little of column A, a little of column B. There's statues everywhere, like they were too heavy to bother with, and some dressers, some beds so big I think they were just assembled inside of the room—they could be there from the 1800's. But your aunt probably knew more than I did—she probably told you stories, right?"

"Oh no—she was always quiet about the place. I think she believed in servant-employer privilege."

"Ha, well. Even if Arthur told anyone anything in town here, there's not so much to tell." Daphne fought back a flush. What if the good people of Hillsdale found out all the things she and the Master had done? Then the boldness she'd had this afternoon with Luke returned to her. *Let them.*

"I'd love to see up there. Especially if the furniture—if you're redecorating, you've got to let me know first. Please don't send anything to the dump—"

"I'd never throw away so much history."

The blonde offered her hand out. "A woman after my own heart. I'm Theo."

"Daphne," Daphne smiled and shook.

"Let me give you my card." She picked one up off of the desk and turned it over to write on the back. "That's my cell phone. Call any time."

"Thank you so much," Daphne said, and meant it. "You're sure your aunt never said anything about the house? Anything at all?"

"She'd never let me up there. It's funny—I was the same age as that girl who died." Theo said, then winced. "You did hear about that, didn't you? I know it was a long time ago—I hope someone told you—oh my gosh—"

"I've been told."

"Oh good, phew." She shrugged helplessly. "Any time I asked my aunt about the place, she just said something about it not being safe. I always assumed it was under construction—you know how big houses are, there's always something needing to be done, loose nails and belt sanders. And I was a pretty hyper kid—maybe she was worried I'd run amuck and break things."

Daphne cast a meaningful glance at all the china in glass display cabinets. "Clearly, a valid fear."

Theo laughed, and Daphne liked the sound of it. It'd been so long since she'd laughed—since she'd had someone to talk to who wasn't Richard or Arthur.

"Come by for lunch tomorrow? If you can take it off, that is—"

Theo's smile grew from ear to ear. "I'll have to ask the boss—oh, wait—that's me."

Daphne grinned. "Twelve—and I promise to give you the full tour."

"Sounds lovely," Theo said, and Daphne waved through the glass window as she left the store.

SHE MULLED over the conversation on her way home, and told Arthur Theo would be coming over for lunch. She pulled out the other woman's business card, and found that it had Theo's last name.

"Did you know a Hetherington?"

"Oh, Mrs. Hetherington? She worked with the new family, exclusively. I'd retired by then—she never knew the Master."

"If they were the new family, what are we Arthur? The new-new family?"

"You're the current family in residence," he said, overly grand, and she snorted lightly.

They arrived at the house, and when she went upstairs to shower and change into clean clothes for dinner, she found that the riding crop was gone.

. . .

MRS. DUDLEY FINISHED MAKING dinner quickly and Daphne ate it just as fast. The second she heard the servants leave and the alarm turn on she ran upstairs to her bedroom and took off all her clothes.

"Where was I last night? Show me?" The riding crop was still missing. Unless Mrs. Dudley's knees had suddenly gotten better, she thought she knew who had it. "I want to see it with my own two eyes."

There was a strange sound from somewhere else in the house. She stilled, wondering if she'd really heard it—if it were mice, or raccoons, or burglars.

The sound came again. Closer now. And the sound of a foot in the hall.

A cracking sound, and she found she could quickly identify it. The sound of leather hitting flesh, steady as a metronome, coming nearer, nearer, the steps louder and closer, until the cracking of the whip and the thump of the man who carried it was right outside her bedroom door.

Daphne's breath caught, trapped again between panic and exhilaration. He would show her where the dungeon was in his own good time—but she had amends to make with him first.

The bedroom door creaked open, but the light inside hardly crept out. She thought she could see him there in the shadow, standing, waiting for her. Animal instincts rose in her, the urge to flee sending a bitter stripe across her tongue. She owed him this, she knew, for her dalliance with Luke, but she was still scared by the prospect of it—and of being cornered in here with him.

So she ran.

She rushed past him at the door, only barely, she felt his heat there, taking up all the room, but she pushed through, and then ran down the hall nakedly—and he chased after her. She could hear his footsteps behind her, three, two, one step behind, and then *thwack*, across her ass. She yelped at the sting, but kept running, in the dark and with whatever moonlight filtered in.

He could have out run her, she was sure of it, and yet he didn't, content to let her race, hitting her with the whip as often as he could. Her heart was pumping, her lungs hot, and her bottom burned each time the crop left a new line.

Eventually she stumbled at the top of the far stair, running bodily into a statue's stand. It teetered precariously and she caught it before it could fall, her current amount of adrenaline enough to haul it back into place.

Her care for his house didn't make him stop though. *Thwack, thwack,* the whip bit into her, and she found herself clinging to the cold angel. He lashed her again, and again, and she cried out into the folds of its angelic robes.

Finally the sound of the whip stopped, and there was only her voice left, the small defeated sounds she was making, even with him holding his hand. Then a clatter, as the riding crop fell to the floor.

She stayed where she was, letting the cool marble soothe her—and then hot hands picked her up. She gasped in surprise as he lifted her, and let out a hiss of pain as he set her sore ass down on the railing over the hall below.

Panic gripped her—she couldn't fight him now, she might fall back and dash her brains on the tile—she hurried to wind her feet in the bars even as his hands were pushing her thighs wide apart. She felt like she might fall and screamed in true fear, until he caught her, one hand around her waist, pulling her back up like she was a dancer dipped too low. Then with his other hand, again, he pushed her legs open, bringing her to the railing's edge, making her show herself to him. His hips spread her inner thighs, and she felt the head of his cock probing in.

Daphne couldn't rock forward or pull away, the railing was narrow and her ass already hurt—all she could do was stay still as he slowly pushed his way inside her.

"Don't let me fall," she whispered as he thrust fully in, pushing her fractionally back. "Please, don't let me—"

She reached for the railing again, and found his hand, not just warm this time but textured too, the feel of skin, the knots of knuckles—more substance than she'd ever felt from him before. Her hand trailed up his arm to find his neck and feel it solid where his shoulders met and slowly, so slowly, she started to hold onto him instead of the railing.

She clung to him, her arms around his shoulders and chest, as his cock slid in and out of her—and then she unwound her legs from the railing and looped them out around his waist, until her feet were intertwined. This was the most solid he'd ever been with her—even moreso when his hands went under her ass and picked her up again.

She whimpered in fear as he hoisted her in midair, seeing nothing in front of her, yet all of her senses telling her she was held, penetrated, owned. He stood in the hallway for the both of them, using his hands to hold her steady as he rocked back and forth into her. She closed her eyes so that she wouldn't think she was insane, so that she could just concentrate on how it felt—her ass was on fire from where the crop had lit against it, and the places where his hands touched her burned, and yet her traitorous pussy needed him. She breathed faster and clung tighter, signaling him to thrust deeper still, and he spun her around until her back was against a wall, pinning her there with his cock. The sound of her voice rose in the open, not constrained by a room, and she heard the open slaps of his body hitting against her wetness just as sharp as the whip had echoed prior.

Everything in her tightened, desperate to be held and to hold onto him, inside and out, until she screamed aloud in satisfaction, the urgency of his thrusts making the sound vibrate.

He sped up after she came, fast, faster, fastest, until he held her still, pulling her down and pushing himself up, and she cried out again for his sake, because he could not, imagining him losing himself inside her.

Then he pulled out of her without setting her down, changing his hold on her to be like a cradle. She didn't question this, just sagged against his chest, in closed-eyed relief, as he took her down stairs, across the tile hall, and up the other stairs to her own bedroom. Once there he flung her on the bed so hard she bounced.

She heard his departing steps heavy in the hall, walking away from her, leaving her all alone on her too big bed.

"Stop!" she called after him, and he did. Heat was radiating from her ass from where he'd whipped her and it reminded her of his hands. "Come back?"

Her voice sounded so small in such a big place. But his steps returned to her, pausing in the door. Willing herself courage, she threw the sheets on the other side of the bed down. "Stay the night?"

Inside her room his steps were silent, and so she wasn't sure if he'd heard her—even if she'd made her request aloud. But she felt the weight of him as he got into the bed, felt the springs sigh and give as he crawled up the bed to get into it behind her and then pull the sheets back up.

Slowly, ever so slowly, she put her back against his chest, and chastely went to sleep.

CHAPTER 17

The alarm chirped, waking her to a still dark room. The curtains were drawn, yes, but no light peeked in from behind them—and Daphne realized with a start that she ought to be afraid. Had Arthur forgotten something and come back? Or had someone jumped him and taken his keys? She scooted back on the bed and found the Master's presence still there. In moments, his heat overcame her chilling fear.

"Daphne?" a man's voice shouted from below. "Pet, dear, I'm home!"

She sagged in the bed. "Richard?"

It was his feet she heard on the stair now. Him, lumbering up in the dark, with his luggage. She reached over and turned on her reading lamp and saw the covers tousled all around her. Three people could be hiding in here with her, not just one ghost.

"It's the middle of the night," she said as he appeared in the doorway.

"I know! I rushed home to see you, as soon as I could."

"You did?"

"Don't I always?" he asked, with a grin.

"And what about your work?"

"The market righted itself again. With me standing beneath it, just like Atlas." He set his bag down and mimed holding the world. Then he started taking off his tie.

She pressed her head into her pillow and pulled the sheets up. "Turn off the light when you're through."

He took his time. She heard him shuffling around their room, kicking his shoes off, brushing his teeth, and then felt him sink into bed, not where he belonged, not back where the Master had been sleeping, but in front of her, pushing her warm sheets up.

"What?" her voice was rough with sleep and prior screaming.

"When I left you couldn't get enough of me." His voice was a low rumble in his chest, and his hands were reaching out for her waist.

"That was before you came home at four a.m., Richard."

"But you made me promise." His hand trailed up her side. "I took a solemn oath to fuck you as soon as I returned," he said as he cupped her breast. "And Vances are always good for their word," he said, lowering his mouth to nuzzle at her nipple.

"You—" she moved to push him away, but—if he wanted her, and if she still wanted a child—she was hovering in indecision, trying to deny how good his suckling felt, when a hot hand touched the middle of her back and ever so slightly pushed her forward, into Richard.

She made a soft noise, and Richard chuckled like he knew her better than she did.

"I hate…when you leave," she said, not sure which part was a lie.

"I know, pet, I know," he bowed to kiss her other breast now, to do that same thing he always did, where he sucked her nipple in and then stroked his tongue across it deliberately inside his mouth, and she shuddered.

Was she betraying the Master by being with him? The hand on her back was insistent, pushing her, daring her to continue.

Richard leaned against her, trying to turn her over so he could cover her, but she quickly shook her head.

"I want it like this." She didn't want to turn over and find the Master gone away.

Richard grinned, smug. The reading lamp cast shadows down on him, making him look like a devil.

"Whatever my pet wants, she gets," he said, pulling himself up the bed, his erection rubbing against her thighs as he rose. He kissed her and she put her leg up over his side, feeling his cock angle down and his hand following it to tilt it to fit inside her.

Despite the all the reasons she had to hate him, Richard fit her perfectly. Perhaps that was why she'd been so willing to overlook his many flaws. When he was inside of her, she felt complete, like a puzzle that's final piece had been found at long last. She moaned as he slid in, and so did he, his cock satisfied to finally be home.

"I could never get tired of fucking you," he said, looking down at her, kissing her face wherever he could reach as his hips began to thrust.

Her pussy gave an involuntary squeeze, knowing that he lied, same as she did when she said, "Nor I, you."

There were no words then for a few moments in time, just them rocking with one another, in and out, dancing in perfect, gasping, time.

And then, from behind her, heat neared anew. She tensed and Richard looked down. "What is it, pet?"

"Nothing," she said, shaking her head quickly.

"Are you sure?" His thrusting slowed.

The Master was right behind her now. She imagined him breathing on her neck, and she could feel his hands caressing her back, her hot ass, her thighs. "What if tonight's the night? That this finally takes?" she said, trying to remind the Master why she was there.

"Then I'd be delighted," Richard said, in a low growl, with another thrust.

As he said the word delighted, the Master spread her ass wide, and she felt his cock slide down her cleft and position itself where he and only he had taken her once before.

She inhaled sharply, but didn't protest, feeling a slight pulling, and then an immediate sense of fullness—oh, God, had she ever been this full before? She clawed her hands on Richard's shoulder as the Master slid inside.

"Go slow, Richard," she begged. "If this is the time—make it count."

Richard blinked and then nodded solemnly. "Okay," he said, and started thrusting anew.

The two of them inside her, one in front and one in back—the sensation of being stretched and nerves lighting up that had never lit before—Daphne started to moan incessantly as the two of them worked at her, dancing between both of them now, pinned and trapped. Richard sped up, unable to help himself.

"Pet," Richard grunted, between thrusts. "You're so hot and tight, it's unreal."

"I know—" Daphne gasped. "Don't stop—"

"I couldn't if I wanted too," he growled in her ear.

Her voice rose as they fought over her sex, her hips in Richard's hands, her breasts in the Master's, and she felt like she was being torn in two by pleasure.

She put her hands up to use the headboard to push down, unable to get purchase on anything else with both of them inside her.

"I'm going to—I can't hold on anymore—" Richard warned her, and she felt his cock stiffen even more inside, as the Master kept ramming into her ass, harder and harder.

"Wait—just—" she flung one hand out behind her and felt the Master's ass there, clenched as he thrust. This was for him, he had to know that, everything was for him—

"I'm coming for you!" she shouted triumphant, her hips spasming between both cocks like a trapped pinball. Everything in her pulled tight, and Richard took her pussy fast, letting it grab his cock.

"Yes, yes, yes," Richard groaned, guttural, sending waves of hot cum deep inside her.

He slid out but the Master stayed deep, claiming her as his own. Then he pulled out too and Daphne sagged, like a puppet bereft of strings.

Richard reached a hand down, and pushed her hair away from her face. "Now *that* is how you make a baby."

Daphne could hardly breathe, but nodded in desperate hope.

CHAPTER 18

Richard, with his iron constitution, was up at dawn the next day to work. Daphne felt him leave the bed and crawled like a cat into the warm spot that he'd left.

The pregnancy tests would arrive today, and then she'd know where she was. Despite his anger after her interlude with Luke, the Master had seemed to understand her predicament last night.

And last night—she ran her hand down her chest, shivering. If only every night could be like that. She closed her eyes, savoring the memories, and then reluctantly got out of bed. Reality called, as did a shower.

She was drying off when Richard came back in.

"Pet!" He was still wearing his robe—he could do all his work at home online—and all the better to jerk off to chats with Becca in.

Daphne made a face at that—and didn't think to cover herself in time.

"Oh my god—what the hell happened to you?" He crossed the room and grabbed her arm so that she had to present her ass to him.

She looked over as though she'd forgotten herself. Yesterday's escapade with the whip had left her marbled black and blue. "I was climbing in the stable yesterday and I fell."

120

Richard looked horrified. "What on earth were you doing climbing?"

"I was trying to see if the wood in the hayloft was rotten or not. I want our baby to have a pony."

"I need you to be safe, pet—what if something had happened to you?" Richard made a face and shook his head. "Besides, our child won't be able to ride until it's three or four."

"I like to think ahead." His concern was charming, and she smiled winningly at him. After last night everything seemed possible again. Maybe there was a way that everything could work. The three of them, and one small child.

He smiled back at her and her heart raced like it used to and then —there. At the corner of his mouth, Daphne could tell something was missing. It was like a fraction of his smile had been stolen away. A piece of him broken off, given to someone else.

She could see him trying to give his whole heart back to her. She'd held all of it once before, she was sure. But now that another woman owned a part of it, it wasn't fully his to give again.

"I do hope things work out," he said, patting gently at her stomach.

"Me too," she said, hollowed out by sadness.

He walked past her on his way in to the bathroom, and Daphne finally glanced at a clock.

"Richard—you'd better put on some pants."

"Why?"

"I invited someone from town up for lunch today."

Richard made a questioning sound as he peed.

"An antiques dealer. Her name's Theo. Her aunt used to work here —I think we should get rid of some of the statues." She said things she didn't mean just to have a reason to talk to him.

"I thought you liked the statues?" A flush and then the sound of the faucet.

"I do, but they're unsafe—I don't want him climbing on them, if we have a boy."

"Climbing up on things—sounds like someone else I know. Hopefully he won't be as clumsy," Richard said.

Daphne bit her lips, holding emotions in. "We can only hope."

DAPHNE WENT DOWNSTAIRS to consult with Arthur and found he'd already set the table for three. "You're perfect, you know that?"

"Thank you, Ma'am," he said with a bow.

Theo arrived precisely at noon, and looked around in awe. "It's even bigger than I thought it was. And the lawns outside—and the trees—"

"I know." Daphne grabbed Theo's hand in a schoolgirl way, excited to finally have someone else to show the house to.

"I can't wait to get the grand tour."

"I can't wait to show you! But lunch first, or Mrs. Dudley will be terribly upset."

DAPHNE AND THEO chatted while eating, and the third place setting sat empty. Richard's work called, which was just as well, she wasn't sure he'd bothered to get dressed yet. It's not like there were any antiques in their bedroom or his office anyhow. She'd just avoid those places and would hope he wouldn't flash Theo. Theo was a little mystified at Arthur's helpful presence.

"He won't bite, honestly," Daphne said. And realized Theo's concerns might be other…. "Also, we're paying him well, I swear."

Theo laughed. "It's not that. It's just that I can't imagine my aunt serving anyone. I mean, she's been a hundred since I was two, so just thinking about her scurrying in and out, carrying plates—" She shook her head to indicate the impossibility.

"She and Arthur didn't overlap—he only served the old family. He came out of retirement for us."

"Old indeed! My aunt only worked here for three years."

"Oh? What happened?" Daphne leaned forward, eager for gossip about the house, even if it was twenty years out of date.

"I have no idea. If she was anything back then like she is now though—I'd guess she probably got fired, after throwing silverware in her purse."

Theo laughed and Daphne laughed, and God, she loved laughing.

Theo stood. "Come on—I want to see it all. The whole thing."

Daphne took Theo through every room, every nook and cranny of the place, except for Richard's office and their bedroom and the dungeon where the Master had taken her, since she still didn't know when that was. Theo inspected everything closely, all the pieces of furniture and statuary, tracing her finger along seams and trying out drawers, occasionally making a satisfied noise.

"Well?" Daphne asked when they were through.

"Well..." Theo said, pursing her lips like she was about to tell Daphne sour news. "The whole house is an amazing example of American primitive."

"What's that?"

"It's homemade art. And furniture, obviously. He knew what he was doing—the drawers pull smoothly, the slats fit together well—but because it's not of a more popular style, or by a famous craftsman, it lacks extrinsic value." Theo walked over and tapped at a statue, and Daphne wondered a little crazily if her actions made it mad. "You can't break it up—they're only worth anything, in context, as a full set here, really. You could sell tickets though, or have open houses—set this place up as a kind of small museum."

"Oh," Daphne said, deflating. "I mean, I wasn't ever going to sell any of it. I was just curious."

"Of course you were!" Theo said. "The lawns are lovely, and you have so many bedrooms—you could turn this place into a bed and breakfast, easy."

Daphne couldn't begin to imagine strangers trampling in and out of the Master's house. "Maybe," she said.

"Do you know anything about the original owner? He must have been a bit of a kook—building and carving so much—it's a crazy labor of love."

I know everything and nothing about him, Daphne longed to say. "Just what I've heard from Arthur. He said the Master was a very stern man, but he only knew him at the end of his life."

"The Master?" Theo's eyebrows rose.

"Arthur's name for him, not mine," Daphne lied, and it tasted bitter on her tongue. "Would you like to see his workshop?"

"Yes, please," Theo clapped her hands, and Daphne led the way out.

THEY WALKED through the fallow vegetable garden, which Theo ooh'd and aah'd over, the sound of lawn mowers in the air. And when they turned around a row of hedges, they ran straight into Luke. They saw him before he saw them, he was trimming back the edges of a bush with the same clippers he'd held when he'd seen her in the window.

"Hello," Theo said, with a bit of a leer, and he looked up, startled. At seeing Daphne, he smiled.

"Hey," he said, lowering his ear-protectors.

Theo veered towards him, instead of staying on the stable's path. Daphne grabbed the other woman's arm and introduced them quickly. "Theo, this is my gardener—gardener, this is Theo." Luke's face clouded at that, and Theo fought her for just a second, before letting herself be dragged back.

FROM INSIDE THE WORKSHOP, the lawn mowers sounded like distant bees. Theo wandered around the small dark room appraisingly. "Well, this only confirms it," she announced, at the end of her circuit, kneeling down to consider the half-formed statue that'd watched Daphne and Luke fuck.

"He was some kind of crazed lone genius…but that's it." She rose up and dusted off her knees and gave Daphne an apologetic smile. "I'm sorry, I know you were hoping it'd be worth a mint—"

"Oh, not really. My husband and I are well off. I was more just curious what we had. I'd never seen anything like it before."

"Neither have I—and I've spent half my life doing this." She glanced at her watch. "I should be getting back to the store."

"I'll take you back," Daphne said, gesturing towards the stairs. Theo took them casually—and three steps from the bottom, fell hard on her ass.

"Oh my gosh!" Theo clung to the wall, staggering back up.

Daphne trotted down quickly. "Are you okay?"

"I just—phew—it's," she looked around herself. "It felt like someone pushed me."

"What?"

Theo crossed her arms, as if protecting her chest. "It was so weird. I could have sworn I felt somebody's hands."

"Are you having a heart attack?" Daphne asked. "Or a stroke?" She fluttered a hand out to Theo's forehead.

Theo ducked down and started playing it off. "No, I'm fine. Just clumsy."

Daphne gave her a pained smile. "I know how that goes."

Daphne took Theo straight through the house, and Theo chattered nervously along the way, worried perhaps that her outburst in the workshop had seemed strange. It would have, if Daphne hadn't known better.

She escorted her to the front door, and opened it up, spotting Theo's car in the driveway.

"Pet! Pet!" Richard called from above. Daphne twisted, and saw him loping down the stairs, two at a time. Luckily, he was dressed. "I wanted to meet your friend."

"You missed lunch," she chided.

"Work—but I'm here now. Richard, owner of this vast estate," he said, introducing himself after reading the landing, with a silly affected bow.

"Theo, owner of the antique store in town," Theo said, bowing back.

"Well, are we unimaginably wealthy, or are we living in rustic squalor?"

Theo's expression was surprised and she inhaled. "I'll explain later, Richard," Daphne said, putting a hand on his arm. "Theo's got to get back."

"Drat. Well, I'm sorry for being rude—you'll have to come back for our dinner party."

"What?" It was Daphne's turn for surprise.

"It's tomorrow night," Richard said, as though he hadn't heard her. "Seven o'clock, if you'd like to come. It'll be casual—as casual anything inside this house can be."

"Thank you—I'd love to attend!" Theo said, and stepped outside, waving at the both of them. "Anytime you want to come and see me in town, please do," she said, with a nod towards Daphne, and then got into her car.

DAPHNE WAITED until the front doors were closed to round on Richard. "Dinner party?"

"I forgot to tell you—I invited half the board over. Everyone wants to see this place."

"But it's not ready yet—the rooms aren't done —"

"Once you're done redecorating, we can have a proper house-warming. This is just going to be a few of the boys and their wives."

"But there's not enough bedsheets!"

"I ordered ten sets of sheets and towels online this morning. They'll get here in time. Just like the other things I saw you order," he said, waggling his eyebrows.

Daphne blanched. When she'd been ordering pregnancy tests is when Becca'd chatted her. Had Becca talked to Richard since?

"We don't even have curtains —"

"We'll string up the extra sheets then." He grabbed her shoulders and squeezed her tight. "Don't worry—I've already warned everyone. It'll be fine."

"If you say so." Frowning, she capitulated again.

. . .

RICHARD RACED back up the stairs, back to 'business', and Daphne walked to the library and looked up at the Master's portrait.

"Why did you push her? That wasn't right." She looked around the room, waiting to feel him. "Was it because she was touching your things? I was never going to sell them. I just wanted to have a friend."

Daphne realized the Master hadn't shoved Theo down the stairs to hurt her badly—he'd just pushed her back up them, and waited until she was almost all the way down first, like a warning. But still—it was frightening.

"I don't like it when you're rude to company."

"Oh really?" a voice behind her asked. She jumped and whirled. Luke stood there, arms crossed in the doorway.

"Good enough to put my cock in you, but not enough to be introduced?" he said as he advanced, shaking his head.

"Shhhh!" she pleaded.

He sliced the air between them with one hand. "This—whatever it was—it's through."

"Please, no—"

"I thought you were different."

"I am. I was just startled. This is the first time I've done anything like this. I don't know how to be—and Richard's home. He came back last night, without telling me."

The cloud over Luke's face lessened as she spoke, giving her the nerve to come near.

"I can't let anything on," she moved to touch his arm, remembering the way it felt around her in the workshop, how strong it had been. "But I'm sorry for embarrassing you. I'm not like the others. I swear."

Luke inhaled and exhaled deeply, blowing air through his nose like a winded horse. "I'm sorry. I just didn't want to be treated like that again."

"I wouldn't." She wanted to touch his face with her other hand, run it up through his hair, and pull his mouth down to hers. Being so near to him—with Richard here, it was dangerous. But at the thought of

Richard's withholding smile this morning—she rocked up onto her toes and kissed him.

He stiffened in surprise, and then he pulled her to him and kissed her voraciously. They both knew it was an awful idea, which was why they kept going—inside the house, the threat of being caught, made every touch burn twice as hot.

Luke put his hands around her waist and picked her up, carrying her across the library towards the massive desk at the far end, under the Master's watchful gaze. *He had to understand, he had to*—Daphne closed her eyes as he lay her down on the ground so they were hidden by the desk and let her body do all the thinking.

Her hands reached for his belt, tugging his pants down, as he shoved her skirt up. She felt like she was proving herself to him, that she wasn't like all those other women who were embarrassed to be seen with him, who never let him inside their fancy homes. She wanted him under this roof—and inside of her.

As he entered her it was hard not to moan. But both of them were being utterly quiet now, so there were only the soft sounds of him mounting her, the slick slide of his cock into her pussy and the light pounding where their flesh met.

One of his hands behind her head cradled it from the hardwood, the other held himself up over her, arm flexed. She looked up, winding her hands in his shirt, sweat dripping down onto her as he sped up. His face was serious, dark, and she realized that he didn't care if she came, this was about him taking his own pleasure from her, conquering her underneath her husband's nose, which perversely made everything hotter, and she started to rock her hips in time with his, his eagerness urging her on to please him, to help him fuck her until he lost himself in her again.

"Please, please, please," she whispered, and he curled down, breath hot in her ear.

"Shh," he warned, and she could feel his cock stiffening, ready to shoot his load.

"Daphne!" Richard's voice boomed from the second floor. "Dapppphnnnneeee...."

Luke's fingers curled into her hair, pulling her head back.

"I'll be right there!" she somehow yelled back up to her husband in a normal voice.

Luke's thrusts became erratic and she knew he was close—as close as she was to getting caught and then—he growled in her ear, fucking her into the floor, so hard it hurt. She bit her lips to stop from whimpering and felt her pussy quiver around him, wanting more as he gasped aloud, rough and harsh in her ear, his cum spilling out inside of her, just as she was so close to coming herself—

"Daphne!" Richard shouted, now from somewhere on the first floor—and Daphne hit Luke's shoulder in frustration. He rose up and pulled out, reaching down to hide his flaccid cock back in his jeans.

"When does he go again?" he asked her, breathing hard.

"There's a dinner party this weekend. Next week, maybe?" Daphne said, rising to kneel, pulling her underwear back up and pushing her skirt down, feeling his hot cum spill between her thighs.

"Good." Luke said, as she stood.

"Hide here until I come back."

He nodded, and tucked himself under the desk.

"There you are, pet!" Richard said, coming into the library. He was in his robe, again.

"Yes, dear?" Daphne said, and smoothed a hand through her hair. "I'm sorry—I was taking a nap." She pointed towards the couch.

"You were tired?"

"Just all of a sudden, yes."

"Do you think…." he said, eyeing her belly.

"I don't know. Yet." She gave him a coy smile and prayed he wouldn't cross the room to her.

"I was thinking about taking a break myself. After last night in particular…." One of his eyebrows rose, and ran a suggestive hand down the front of his robe.

It was her—and Luke's—easiest way out.

And—*heaven help her*—her body was still hungry.

"Race you to the bedroom —" she said, and turned, running down the library's back hall.

She only beat him to the bedroom because he wanted her to win—all the better for her purposes. The second he got in the door she flung herself at him, shedding clothing, hoping that the remaining scent of Luke would fall away with them. And when they fell to the bed together, kissing, he whispered, "You're so wet again," without suspicion.

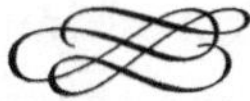

CHAPTER 19

Daphne came twice for Richard. The first time was Luke's really, the orgasm he'd stoked inside her still lay in wait like a coiled snake, only waiting for the chance to strike. Four strokes in, and her clit rubbing against Richard's stomach and she was thrashing in the bed for him, making him feel masterful over her. He stayed still, relishing the feeling of her pussy milking his cock, and then he took his time, believing himself to have already conquered. It made him more patient than usual, thinking that he'd turned her that on, taking all of the pressure off of him.

Instead he wanted to enjoy himself in her. He sped up and slowed down, kissed her nipples, and rose up between her legs to stroke his thumb at her clit. She didn't want to come again for him, yet he rode her with such easy familiarity and she let herself be ridden—her hips twitched without thinking and the muscles of her belly tightened. And when he realized her second time was near he was like a child unable to stop himself from putting his hand into a flame, he was intent on drawing it from her, he wouldn't stop until he had.

So when she shouted, "Oh God!" loud enough for anyone still in the house to hear, Daphne couldn't really feel like she'd betrayed anyone, it was more like he'd brought her body home.

He purred to himself to see it, and then finished himself in her, his seed mixing with Luke's inside, before rolling off of her and grinning at the ceiling.

"I love you, pet," he told her.

"I love you, too," she told him back.

DAPHNE REASSEMBLED herself much more slowly than Richard did. Five minutes of snuggling then a shower, and he was gone, markets had opened somewhere in the world and he needed to be ready. She crawled out of their bed, knowing she ought to be ashamed of herself, for everything, but unable to mount a proper response. She showered, and made her way back down to the library. Luke wasn't behind the desk anymore. Of course not—he'd probably left as soon as she had, once he'd realized what she'd gone off to do.

She leaned against the desk and looked at the floor, felt the space he'd left inside of her, the wetness of his cum despite her recent rinsing, and then she looked up at the Master's portrait, staring silently down.

"What have you made of me?" she asked it.

Nothing, she realized, that she hadn't wanted to make herself.

She pushed away from the desk and went back upstairs.

SHE WAS READING a book in bed that evening when Richard finally arrived.

"How was work?"

"Hard."

"It's hard to take that seriously when you're wearing a robe."

"The sheets and the tests, should arrive tomorrow morning, and guests should start getting here around six tomorrow night."

"Who are they?"

"Glenn, Roger, James, Tyler and their wives —."

"Why now? Why haven't I met them before?"

"You're the one who wanted to elope," Richard said, tweaking the end of her nose.

Daphne bit her lips. She hadn't wanted a wedding when she didn't have any family to attend.

"But they all want to meet you, and see our new house. Glenn wants to be a godfather to our baby."

"You've told them?"

"Why wouldn't I?"

"It's private!"

"How we make the baby is private. The rest of it most certainly is not. Soon you'll waddle into town and strangers will be petting your belly."

"Ugh. I can imagine nothing worse." She rolled over, burying her nose in her book. Richard sidled into bed behind her, and she expected him to take up his own book, like he did most nights that he was home—so she was surprised to feel his hand against her back.

"Yes?" she twisted to look over her shoulder at him.

"Shouldn't we go again?"

Daphne made a face at him. "We already did this afternoon—once a day should be enough, Richard."

"Technically," he agreed. But he pushed the sheet down over the curves of her body and started pushing her tank top up. "But isn't more often, better?"

Daphne made a disagreeable sound. "Richard —"

He brought his body in line with hers, shoulders to shoulders, knees to knees, hips to hips. She could feel the outline of his cock against the cleft of her ass. He leaned in and whispered, "Ever since we moved here, I just can't get enough of you." His hands sank to her waist and started pushing her underwear down.

"Richard," she protested.

"Pet," he said, rubbing himself against her closed thighs, his voice low. "You have to let me in, pet. I need to fuck you now."

A weight dropped between Daphne's legs again and started rolling in time with the head of his cock. His hand reached over her, under her shirt, for her breast. "Pet—pet, I've got to fuck you." He rolled her nipple between thumb and forefinger, giving it a tug.

Without thinking, Daphne started to lift her leg to let him in. He took advantage of her weakness and leaned forward into her, pushing her onto her stomach as her legs began to spread. His cock probed between her thighs, once, twice, and then he found the right angle to catch himself into her.

"Oh God," he whispered, sliding himself home. "There's something about this bedroom pet—seeing you lying on this bed—you're irresistible to me." He put a hand on either side of her shoulders to hold himself up as he started to thrust in and out of her. "I can't rest until I'm buried—deep—inside—you," he said, punctuating each word with a thrust. Daphne groaned, taking him in, reaching a hand between her legs to touch her clit.

"You have no idea how good you feel," he said. "I need you so much."

Richard hardly ever spoke during sex—which was too bad, because everything he said now was turning her on. Daphne started breathing in time with him, arching her hips up so that he could go deeper.

"It's been so long," he whispered, hoarse.

"It's only been a few hours, Richard," Daphne corrected him, closing her eyes, trying to let go and roll with the moment.

"A few hours without this feels like a lifetime." He was taking broad strokes into her now, deep, his whole body lying practically on top of hers, pinning her down. He made a frustrated growling sound and leaned back, pulling out, and yanked her to all fours. She yelped in surprise at being manhandled, and felt him push his way back inside her. "I've got to have this again," he said, holding her hips still so that he could thrust wildly.

"Richard!" she protested—more out of surprise than anger. Her husband wasn't the passionate one, never said those sorts of things, and—a hand lifted up from her hip and slapped across her ass. "Richard!" This time she yelled for real.

Daphne fell forward and squirmed away from her, glaring back at him over her shoulder. "What was that?"

"What was what?" He was staring down at her, baffled, looking foolish on his knees with his straining cock.

"You hit me."

"Did I?" Richard looked around the bed as if amazed to be there.

"You did!"

He looked at himself, mystified. "So?"

"So—I don't like it." *At least not from you.* "And I'm already bruised. You saw that earlier."

He inhaled to defend himself, ready to bluster like usual, then deflated as his cock bobbed down. "So I did. Apologies."

"Let's just go back to sleep, all right?" Daphne pulled her shirt down and her underwear back up. Richard nodded agreement, falling back onto his side of the bed. She lay down, facing away from him as she had been earlier.

"I'm sorry, pet," he said, patting her arm like you would comfort a distant cousin, not a wife.

"It's okay," she said, even though it wasn't.

RICHARD WAS up before her in the morning again, chasing after another market.

What had ever given him the idea to spank her? What on earth had made him think that that was going to be all right? Was it the sight of her ass already covered in bruises? Or—something different, something so frightening, she couldn't possibly give it a name?

He arrived in the dining room carrying boxes just as she finished her breakfast, and he seemed completely himself again.

"Sheets for all the beds—or to be used as curtains. There's more in the hall. I'd forgotten how big comforters were."

Daphne's eyebrows rose. How many bedrooms did their house have? "Well, now I know what I'll be doing all afternoon. Did…other things come?"

He shook his head and gave her a sly smile. "Not yet. Odd shipping delay. Perhaps they'll get here by this evening?"

"Perhaps."

"Regardless, no wine for you, just in case." He leaned out and touched his finger to her nose. "I'll have to go into town. I trust Arthur with the menu, but my friends have particular tastes in liquors. I might have to go a few towns over to get a respectful bar set up."

Daphne nodded, watching his face closely. Did he seem different now? Had he changed? "Richard—about last night…."

He made a face and shook his head. "Let's just never mention it again."

"Fine."

"I've got another hour or two before I can take off."

"I'll grab Arthur and start making the rounds with these, then."

"Thanks, pet—you're a gem." He leaned in to kiss her cheek briefly, then set back off to his office upstairs.

DAPHNE LUGGED a matching set of bedding to each bedroom, and all the assorted carved beds inside. She could feel the Master watching her—she couldn't help but bend over, again and again, tucking in so many sheets.

A hot hand pushed her in the third bedroom—the one furthest away from the office, on the far side, the one where he'd taken her ass.

"Don't. He's here. It's disrespectful."

Heat pushed her back against one of the bed's posters, landed against her throat, started reaching up her thigh.

"Did you do something to him last night?" She reached forward and could feel him in front of her, his lips at her collar bone, wrap her arm tentatively around his back. He was becoming more tangible by the minute. "Did you talk to him? Tell him what to do? Or…."

The Master couldn't talk to her—unless they used the computer. This afternoon, when Richard left—

"Stop—I mean it." She pushed the ghost away from her and felt the resistance of his body as she did so. Then she felt his presence leave the room and all that remained was a lingering sensation of heat.

"I'M OFF, PET." Richard found her shortly after lunch. "Hopefully I won't have to go far, but," he jingled his car keys in his hand, indicating a possible journey for decent booze.

Daphne smeared a hand across her sweaty forehead. The house had been fine for her and Richard, but not fine enough for company—and Arthur really was too old to dust. "That's fine. Take your time. Drive safely."

"Will do." He leaned over and pecked her cheek again, before heading out the front door.

Daphne listened to his car go and counted to sixty before going up the stairs to his office.

SHE SAT down in front of the computer and brought up a blank screen. "I know that you're here," she announced to the room. "It's not like you have anything better to do."

Nothing happened. "Come on." She bit her lips and sighed. "I need to know. Was last night Richard...or was it you? You can tell me. Just type it out." She pointed at the keyboard.

She waited for her techno-ouija board to work for a full minute, feeling increasingly foolish—and then a chat window opened up.

You're back! Where've you been?

Becca. Again. Goddammit.

Daphne forgot about the ghost and put her fingers on the keyboard. *"Go away you awful whore."* She typed the words out, but didn't hit return—she'd realized she could scroll up.

She spun the wheel on the mouse and hours after hours of chat logs appeared. These were all recent, in the past few days. Becca's husband must be even more of a rube than she'd been.

They were explicit, too. Descriptions of intimate acts—things

Richard had never even done with her—Daphne sat there reading, stunned.

How had he had this much emotion for someone else? Maybe it wasn't the Master's fault—maybe it was Becca that'd finally set him free.

But if he was in love with Becca, why was he fucking her so hard? And why did he'd tell her he wanted a child?

Daphne copied and pasted everything over into another file and emailed it to herself. More munition for their future divorce, if needbe.

She scrolled back down to the end of the chat, where Becca had typed a few more sentences.

Guess I missed you, baby. But I want to be with you forever, too. See you soon!

Daphne turned the computer off with a frown.

By the time Richard got back in the late afternoon, all the bedrooms were as done as they were going to be.

"Pet, dear—help me carry things in."

Richard had not just bought liquor—he'd purchased an entire store. "How many people are you having over tonight?"

"A few—enough—whoever shows up." He started arranging bottles on the desk in the library, turning it into a make-shift bar. "They're going to spend the night, so I had to buy extra. I don't want anyone sobering up before they have to."

Daphne's lips twisted at that, but they were *his* friends. *He* could deal with them. "I'll get Arthur to bring a tray of glasses in here, and an ice bucket when it's time."

"Good. See if he can bring the martini shaker too? Assuming the kitchen's unpacked."

"I'm sure it is."

If the desk weren't so overly large, like all the other furniture in the house, there was no way it'd hold all the bottles Richard'd gotten, muchless the glassware. The Master's portrait looked down, still unhappy, as Richard brought a bottle of brandy out of a bag.

"Since when do you drink brandy?"

Richard shrugged. "I don't—but someone else might want some."

Daphne inhaled to ask if he'd buy a gold toilet too, using that same principle, but the sound of the phone ringing cut her off. Richard blanched.

"I'll get it," he said, practically running for the door.

Becca. Daphne ground her teeth together—until Richard shouted from the other room. "It's for you!"

Daphne walked out, maintaining her composure, and took the proffered phone from Richard's hand. "Hello?"

"Daphne! It's Theo—from the antique store?"

"Of course!" She cupped her hand over the receiver to tell him, "It's Theo, from yesterday."

Richard nodded, and went back to the library.

"I'm sorry to give you such late notice, but I won't be able to come tonight."

"Oh, that's fine—it was late notice for us to even ask you."

"It's just," Theo started, and then laughed nervously at the far end, "I spoke to my aunt."

Daphne perked up. "Really? What did she say?"

Theo sighed. "Well, she's old, and remember her memory's not what it used to be—but she said the girl who lived there had severe mental disorders, from even when she was a child. It made her see things, and talk to people who weren't there. She did it all the time, my aunt heard her, said it was like she had an invisible best friend."

"Like kids do," Daphne said, trying to explain things away.

"Yes, but hers never went away. My aunt would hear her talking to herself when she walked outside her room, when she was a teenager. I mean, she was clearly crazy, which was why her folks kept her locked up there—but my aunt said the girl never wanted to leave the place, either. Between the therapy and the medications they put her on— they wound up having to keep her to herself most times. That's why they hired tutors for her, they didn't want her to leave the house and go out to school.

"But then she started riding that horse, and going out to horse shows—my aunt said she really came out of her shell, and almost had a normal life. She was even finally talking about going off to college, when the horse spooked and threw her. It's a shame, really. She was such a pretty thing, and so messed up inside her head."

"Wow." Daphne bit her lips in thought. Had…the Master…no, he couldn't have…could he?

Theo sighed on the far end of the line. "My aunt said she'd only talk to me if I promised her one thing."

"What was that?"

"To never to go into your house again."

"Oh come on," Daphne said with a snort. "Why?"

"Too many bad memories. She just doesn't want me to go there."

"It's not like she'll know. I promise *I* won't tell her."

Theo snorted. "It sounds crazy, I know. But I'm a woman of my word—and also I work on Saturday mornings."

Daphne nodded reluctantly, even though the other woman wouldn't see it. "All right."

"I do still want to be your friend, Daphne. I hope this doesn't mess that up—we get so few new people to talk to in town. I can't wait to hear all about your party afterwards, at lunch sometime this week."

"Tuesday?" Daphne offered. By then all of Richard's friends should be gone.

"Tuesday," Theo said, sounding relieved.

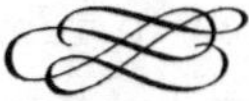

CHAPTER 20

Daphne went upstairs to shower and found Richard already standing inside, singing a song she didn't know. She looked down at the tile, remembered kneeling there, feeling the Master's cock at the back of her throat....

"Care to join me?" Richard asked, peeking out from behind the curtain and then ducking back.

"I'd only get you dirty."

"Do you think I'd mind?" he said. His voice—it was his but it sounded deeper. Rougher. "I could help you polish that bruise off of your ass. There's a lot of soap in here."

No. His voice was all his. She hadn't heard anything strange.

"I'll wait for my turn, thanks," she said, slowly backing out of the bathroom.

DAPHNE TRIED TO LOOK POLISHED, but not too polished. She put on a spring dress, brightly colored, enough make-up to make her look older, but not harsh, and low heels that tapped the floor of every room she walked through, as though she were a prancing horse.

Guests began arriving at six. All of them insisted on helping with their bags after seeing Arthur. They seemed nice enough, although flustered from their assorted journeys, and everyone immediately availed themselves of the bar.

"Glenn, this is Daphne," Richard began, and introduced her to everyone, in a blur of names. Glenn's wife, Sharon, was an imposing figure, twice Daphne's size in every direction, neck completely obscured by pearls, and Roger with his wife Tiffany, and James with his wife Patricia. Daphne tried to remember them all, she'd heard Richard talk about them before, but it was hard to keep track of them when they were all so intense and wore so much black.

Arthur escorted the last wave back down the stairs from their bedroom. Tyler and his wife Naomi. Naomi gave Daphne a quick smile—she was the only one who looked as nervous as Daphne was.

"This place is positively quaint, Richard," Glenn announced, having settled into a glass of wine.

"You said it was a strange, but this?" One of the other men shook his head.

"Nonsense. This is an up and coming area, and you all know it. Are we all here?" Richard asked, taking control of the conversation again. "Do we all have drinks?" Men and women lifted up their glasses. "Then let's go on the tour!" Richard announced, and led them out of the library like they were an upscale pirate band.

Daphne tagged along at the back of the group, and listened to Richard narrate the trip. He told them of how he'd found the place on an obscure real estate listing, like the owners hadn't even really wanted to sell it, but how when he'd come here his first time through—without Daphne—he'd fallen in love. He had a story for each room already—what it had been, what it would be when they were done with it, and Daphne realized he was making everything up on the fly. Her husband, the expert at spin.

It'd worked on her, hadn't it?

For her part, every time they changed rooms, she remembered what the Master had done to her there. The hallways that they'd fucked in, the statue that she'd clung to as he'd whipped her, the massive four-poster where he'd first taken her ass now ceded to

Glenn and Sharon. Her passion with the ghost infused every space in this house—all the times she'd posed for him, gone looking for him, been waiting for him—how could everyone else not feel it?

She felt a warmth behind her—like a hand, cupped against her ass, and turned quickly. Her imagination? Or him, reminding her he was there?

Naomi stood beside her, as the men talked of freshening drinks before dinner. "How can you live here?"

"Excuse me?" Daphne blinked.

"With so many eyes looking at you all the time?" She pointed at the nearest statues. "It's horrifying."

Daphne's jaw dropped, unable to defend herself. "Naomi, don't be rude," Tyler chastised her, and pulled her away, before Daphne could answer.

Arthur had the entire table set by seven. There were ten of them, and she and Richard were at opposite ends of the table, so that they could look down on all their dinner guests like royalty. Naomi was on one side of her and Sharon on the other, with Patricia and Tiffany after them, so that one half of the table was women and the men were free to talk 'business'.

"You'd think they get enough of that during the work week," Naomi said, with a small frown.

"Does your husband travel as often as Richard?" Daphne asked. "By which I mean, a lot. Like half the time."

"Yeah. We got married a few months ago—I only see him on the weekends, really."

"Glenn doesn't travel often enough," Sharon said.

"I thought he traveled with Richard?" Daphne asked.

"Oh, he does. I just wish he were gone more." Sharon gave both of them a pursed smile, and took another sip of her wine. "So what are we going to do with the rest of our weekend here? What entertainments do you have planned?"

Daphne's mouth opened. "I thought everyone was just spending a night. There'll be breakfast tomorrow, of course —"

"We're going to be here for two nights—and I didn't see a TV in our bedroom. A place this big—do you have croquet? Badminton?"

"There's the library."

Sharon gave her a sour look. "It'll have to do, I suppose."

"I like to read," Naomi said, trying to help. Daphne gave her a quick smile—and Arthur emerged from the kitchen with the first course.

SALAD, soup, and finally steak, all of it impeccable. Richard's associates were suitably impressed and the table was littered with the bottles of wine they'd wrested away from Arthur over the course of the evening.

Laughter percolated up from the men's side. "Come on. Somebody's got to have a cigar—Tyler—you're usually good for a Cuban. Don't hold out on us now," Glenn was saying, and sure enough, cigars were pulled out. Sharon fluttered at this, saying something about asthma, using that as an excuse to go outside.

Daphne glared down the length of the table "It'll stay in the walls, Richard."

"It doesn't matter if it stays in the walls. We own them."

Daphne frowned. Alcohol would have helped her impression of this night immensely. She looked around the room at the slurring men, gesticulating wildly with their half-thought ideas, and the women who either whispered to one another—surely unkind things about her or the house—or hovered near the men, trying to be included in their conversation, and again, even in a room full of people, Daphne felt incredibly alone.

Then underneath the table a hand reached up and touched her inner thigh.

She gasped, but no one heard her. She tried to close her legs, but hands as strong as steel pushed her knees back open, and the sensation of heat, of probing fingers, moved higher.

She almost said the word *Stop* aloud. But what if anyone else at the table heard her? What would they think?

What would she tell them anyhow? The truth? No one would believe her. The only other sober person here had been Arthur, and he'd left an hour ago.

She fought the Master with her thighs, trying to hide herself from him. She would have excused herself, only what was the point, where could she hide? Daphne licked her lips and realized the enormity of her predicament.

There was no place in the house where she could be away from *him*. No where *he* couldn't follow her.

He wasn't just the Master of the house now—he was the Master of her.

It was frightening and impossibly erotic at the same time. She was as trapped here with him as she had been in the dungeon, bent over, chained. Slowly, ever so slowly, she gave in.

He spread her knees wide beneath the table, hands reaching up her thighs. Sensing that she'd abandoned herself to him, he started in on her, using a finger to pull the fabric of her underwear aside and another to massage the entrance of her pussy—he wasn't content just to have his way with her, he wanted her to enjoy it to, he was going to make sure that she came here, in front of so many other people, she wouldn't have a choice....

All these people here thought she didn't matter—they'd almost ignored her completely, except for politeness's sake. Little did they know what was happening to her underneath the table's edge, how the Master's fingers were rubbing inside of her, how insistent his thumb was on her clit, how much he wanted to own her right under their very noses, how much he wanted her to come.

She tried not to think about what was happening to her, and it felt as though she were pulled in two—the drab ignorable housewife above, the incandescent woman hidden underneath. She clutched at the edge of the table, her knuckles turning white, she could feel her face flushing, her nipples harden, her wetness soaking through her underwear and likely staining her chair, and—and—and—she came. In quiet shudders that would have looked like moments of distraction to anyone else, biting the insides of her lips, pleasure pulled from her body, spooled onto the Master's hands below.

When she was done she sagged forward, leaning on her elbows, looking like one of the very drunk men, and thunder clapped outside as rain began.

Sharon turned to look at her. "Now's when you'll find out all your house's dirty secrets."

"What?" Daphne flushed with guilt.

"All the shit the realtor and inspector didn't tell you about. All the leaks and floods." Sharon seemed pleased that the very house might wash away around them, as though it would serve someone like Daphne right.

"Oh. Yes. That," Daphne limply agreed.

CHAPTER 21

ouples bowed out one by one—and then the lights flickered,
encouraging everyone else to disperse, while they could still
find their rooms. Daphne busied herself taking their dishes into the
kitchen to give Mrs. Dudley a headstart on morning's breakfast.

"Meet you upstairs, pet?" Richard asked, with a leer.

"Soon," she promised him. He was so drunk chances were he'd be
asleep the second his head hit the pillow.

Once she was the only one still up, the house felt like hers again.
She cleared the last of the wine bottles away—Richard did know the
compunctions of his friends, apparently—and washed her hands in
the sink before heading back to the entry way, past the library.

The lights were off, but lightning flashes illuminated through the
library's uncurtained windows, and she thought she saw a figure
standing there. She walked in on tip-toes.

"Is it you?" she asked, breathless.

"I don't know. Is it?" a drunken voice answered her.

Another lightning flash, and she saw Glenn there, holding a snifter
of brandy, looking not unlike the Master's portrait. "Your bedroom's
upstairs."

"I know. I couldn't sleep. Jet lag." He leaned against the desk, which had half as many bottles on it as when the party'd started. He set the brandy down. "Keep me company?"

Daphne took a step backwards, and shook her head. "I'm sorry. I've had a long day, and I'm tired."

Glenn strode across the room to her before she could escape. "I saw you. Looking at me all night. You're a minx, I can tell."

Daphne shook her head, but he was right beside her. Lightning struck and she could see that he'd untucked his shirt, and thunder clapped, and the sound of rain redoubled—she could barely hear him talking, she knew no one would hear her scream.

"Richard's told me about you. The way your face lights up when you get fucked. He says you're the world's best lay. And when someone like him, who's put his cock into every piece of pussy this side of Burma, says that to someone like me—what's he think that's going to get him?" Glenn grabbed her arm as she tried to take another step back.

"You don't want to do this, Glenn."

"Oh yes, I do. I've been thinking about it all night. I know exactly what I want." He pulled her to him as she struggled.

"No!" She thrashed, but he was as big as Richard was, and whereas Richard had never hurt her until last night, Glenn seemed to be familiar with giving others pain. His hands were tight on her arms and he dragged her across the room towards the couch. "Richard! Richard!" she shouted—but the rain—lightning flashed again and she saw the portrait of the Master looking down. Glenn shoved his hand between the two of them, trying to free himself to fuck her.

"Master!" she shouted, in desperation, just as Glenn's knee wedged between her thighs.

Heat rushed over the both of them like a wave of the thunder booming outside, and Glenn's body flew across the room to strike the desk.

Daphne panted on the couch for a moment, pulling herself together, sniffing back tears. Thunder boomed overhead, rattling the windows, making the house shake just like she'd been shaking.

"Oh my God." Daphne sat up and looked over to the floor. Glenn groaned and a dark pool of blood began leaking out from underneath his head where he'd landed.

She screamed.

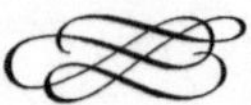

CHAPTER 22

No one heard her.

She didn't stop screaming until she got Richard up, and until he'd gone downstairs to call 911.

"What's wrong?" Naomi appeared in the hallway, and Daphne screamed again—dressed in a white slip, the woman looked like a ghost.

"Glenn—he tried to rape me!"

Naomi blanched even whiter, and then turned and ran.

"You cannot tell them that," Richard said, cupping the phone receiver after having given 911 their address.

"But —" Daphne protested, feeling fragile.

Richard made a face, encouraging her to close her mouth—and behind him, Daphne could see Sharon advancing, like an oncoming freight train,

"You little slut," Sharon tried to slap her across her face, but Tyler reached out over Daphne's shoulder and stopped her.

"Why would he try to sleep with her, when he could have me?" she asked him, still trying to yank her hand down.

"He didn't try to sleep with anyone. I'm sure it was all an epic mistake. Wasn't it, pet?" Richard's eyes begged her to deny the whole thing.

Daphne looked up at Richard, eyes glaring. How dare he tell her that she hadn't been in danger—he wasn't there! If the Master hadn't saved her...who would have?

"Look, he slipped and fell. That's it." Richard was fighting his inebriation, trying to get everyone on the same page before authority arrived, setting the phone down.

"Where is he? I need to see him!" Sharon yelled.

"He's in the library." Daphne pointed to the room's door on the other hall. Sharon pulled her hand back, and started towards it. Daphne watched her go, until Richard took hold of her shoulders and shook her.

"He was just drunk, and you were helping him up to his room. That's what happened." He shook her again, harder than she hoped he meant to. By now everyone else was in the hall around them, and Sharon had started wailing at the sight of her downed husband.

"That's what happened," Daphne repeated dutifully back.

SHE RAN upstairs after that and sat in the middle of her bed like it was an island. The door was open so she could hear the commotion burbling up from below. Was Glenn...dead? She hadn't wanted him to touch her, but did he really deserve that? But if the Master hadn't saved her, it was clear what would have happened.

"Thank you," she said aloud, knowing the ghost would hear.

Heat surrounded her in an instant. The arms of a man around her, burning hot. She bit her lips and rocked back into him, still frightened, and he pulled her tight. And then his hands began to wander.

"No." She pushed at him, shoving him away, but arms came back. "Not you too." She lurched out of the bed, holding herself. "Stop it. This isn't how I want things to be."

Heat remained around her, still for a moment of time—and then left her as though she'd been dipped into an ice bath, and the bedroom door slammed, making her jump.

Had he closed it behind him? Or was he still in here, with her?

Footsteps ran up the outside hall. "Pet?" Richard pushed his head in. "The medics want to know if you need to go to the hospital."

She knew what he was asking. Was she hurt? Even if she couldn't tell any of his friends.

"I'm fine." *Everything's broken and wrong, Glenn, me, you, this house, the Master,* she thought, but swallowed the words without saying them.

RICHARD CAME BACK UPSTAIRS SOON after that.

"Is he alive?" she asked, sitting with her knees under her chin, her arms laced around her legs.

"So far. But he's injured, badly. I don't think you could have hit him harder if you'd had a frying pan."

"I didn't hit him. He tripped and fell."

"Were you…doing anything?"

She wouldn't meet his eyes. "Are you honestly asking me that?"

"He's my oldest friend.…"

"Who said you'd slept with every woman this side of Burma."

Richard made a troubled face. "He shouldn't have said that."

"Is it true?" Her voice was so small. Even though she already knew the answer, she didn't want him to lie to her.

He put a hand to his forehead. His breath still stank like tonight's wine and she suspected he was still a little drunk, because he actually told her the truth. "I may have not been the most faithful husband, pet. But—I love you." He took her wrist in his hand. "And I've sworn off all other women but you. You're the only one for me now. You're going to be the only one for me for forever."

She turned towards him and searched his eyes. She'd seen the chat logs from him and Becca just hours earlier. But he sounded so sincere right now—and despite everything she still wanted to believe him. She needed someone on her side. And maybe for once, he was telling the truth, and it wasn't too late for them to start over.

Tears welled up and she started to sob.

"Oh pet, pet," Richard said, taking Daphne into his arms. "I'm so sorry pet. Glenn's dead to me. Even if he doesn't die tonight."

He held her just like the Master had and she sagged into him.

SHE CRIED ALL the tears she'd been holding back since discovering his betrayal, and when she was done she'd come up with a plan.

"We have to leave, Richard. I don't want to live here anymore."

"Don't let Glenn ruin things for you—you said he didn't touch you, right?"

"We have to pack up right now. We just need to go." Daphne nodded, stronger and stronger, with the wisdom of her decision. "Let's just take a few things, leave the rest of it behind. I feel like this place is haunted, Richard. We just need to start over. Just us. You and me."

Richard's face was disparaging. "Pet, listen to yourself. You're sounding crazy."

"I don't care!" She struggled free of his arms. "I want to leave here. I want to go now and never come back here again!"

Richard caught hold of her arms, gently and folded them back down. "We have guests. And it's raining. We can't go anywhere right now." He was still a little drunk, but she knew he was right.

"Tomorrow?"

"Tomorrow."

"As soon as they leave."

He brought her hand to his mouth and kissed it like a prince. "The second they're gone."

"Okay." She bit her lips and crawled under the sheets. "I want you to stay right here." She dragged him down to lay directly behind her in bed and he went with her. "And don't move the whole night."

"Okay." He nodded into her shoulder agreeably, and soon he was asleep. Daphne willed herself to sleep shortly thereafter.

.   .   .

"Come on, pet." Richard shook her gently in the morning. They were in the same position they'd been in the prior night. Daphne's entire right side felt stiff.

She blinked awake. "We're still leaving, right?"

He nodded. "After we get the guests out."

"As fast as possible."

Daphne went downstairs, holding Richard's hand like he was her new lucky charm.

Arthur had set a sideboard for breakfast, and Naomi was already picking at a plate when they got there. She looked up as they entered. "Any word?"

Daphne wiped a hand across her face. "None yet."

"Sharon didn't call?"

"I don't think she's the calling type," Richard said, cutting her line of inquiry off. "We'll drop by the hospital on our way out today," he said, squeezing Daphne's hand. She squeezed his hand back.

"James and Roger already left—they've got to go to Paris."

"Of course," Richard said, as though their departing without good-byes was expected.

"We'd check in, but we've got a flight to catch too," Tyler announced. He was already in a suit and looked halfway out the door. He picked up a plate and started serving himself eggs.

Some unspoken protocol required that they eat breakfast together, despite how awkward it was. Arthur hovered attentively, trying to discern what'd happened to the missing couple, and why things were so generally unpleasant. He looked to Daphne with a question on his face, and she subtly shook her head.

"Well, that was lovely. Thank you for your hospitality," Naomi said in a perfunctory fashion, once she and Tyler were done.

"Can I bring your bags down, Sir?" Arthur asked.

"No need—I brought them down already," Tyler said, standing and replacing his chair under the table. "Richard," Tyler said, giving him a strong handshake. "Daphne," he said, with a nod.

"I hope you both have a nice trip home," Daphne said, as Tyler drew Naomi away, and waved weakly as they headed to the door.

. . .

THE SECOND she heard the front door close, she dragged Richard upstairs. "Let's go."

"Where to?"

"I don't care." Daphne yanked down half of her closet and shoved it into a bag. Enough clothing for at least two weeks, and she knew she could always buy more.

"Pack for me, too?" Richard said.

"Why?" She didn't want him to leave her sight—and she didn't want to be alone.

"I've got to get some files off the computer. I can work almost anywhere, but I am going to have to work." He reached forward and stroked her chin. "Someone has to bankroll our escape."

They'd leave faster if they could split up—but she was scared to be alone with the Master. "Hurry?"

"For you? Of course."

SHE REACHED into Richard's closet next, throwing heaps of his clothing into a moving box. Three suits, ties, shirts, socks, she didn't check to see if everything matched, she didn't care.

The sound of rain got worse outside, matching her mood more with each second that passed. She ran down to the entry hall with her own bag, and then returned to pick up Richard's box. Daphne wondered what responsibility she had to say good-bye to the Master. She didn't want to be with him again, she wanted things with Richard to work out, but he had rescued her last night—

She opened up her mouth to speak, and then thought better of it. She grabbed Richard's box and pulled the bedroom door shut behind herself.

RICHARD MET her in the entry way with a briefcase.

"Going somewhere?" Arthur asked, looking between them, genuinely confused.

"On a trip," Richard said, with a grin, as though this were just another adventure.

Arhtur's eyebrows rose. "Might I inquire how long you two will be gone?"

"As long as it takes."

"For…what? If I may ask?"

"You may—but I don't rightly know. But my wife wants to leave, and leave we shall. We'll let you know when we return." Richard took her hand in his and squeezed it again.

"If that's the case, may I request permission to leave for Mrs. Dudley and myself, before the weather gets worse?"

"Of course," Richard said grandly. Arthur cast one last worried look at her, but Daphne smiled, and he nodded back, more settled.

She turned to face the door, Richard's hand still in hers. This was it. They were leaving. So close to being free of this place and starting over.

Daphne reached forward and opened up the front door and found a drenched woman standing outside, about to press the doorbell.

CHAPTER 23

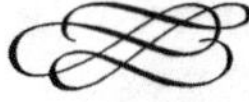

She looked surprised to see them—as surprised as Daphne was to see her.

"Richard?" she said.

"Becca?" His hand fell away from Daphne's. "What are you doing here?"

"You invited me!" Her eyes flickered over Daphne again. "What is *she* doing here? You said she would be gone."

Richard looked horrified. "I said no such thing!"

Despite the fact that Daphne knew precisely who Becca was, she couldn't help but ask, "Who is she?"

Richard looked between the women. She could see his mind whirling, trying to come up with an acceptable explanation, one that would work for the both of them.

He wound up falling to his knees, facing her. "Pet—she's from my past. I meant what promised you last night."

"From your past? I spent two thousand dollars getting here overnight!" the woman protested.

"Why the hell would you do that?" Richard snapped at her.

"You told me to!" Becca looked both wounded and confused.

"We're going," Daphne said, dragging Richard outside.

"You can't just leave me here, Richard," Becca begged.

"Arthur will take care of her, if we tell him." *But would the Master?*

Richard stood between the two women, clearly torn. "We can't just abandon her like that."

"Oh, so it's fine to abandon me for her, but not the other way around?"

Richard's eyes squinted. "Did you know about her?" He sounded offended.

"Don't you dare try to make this about me!" Daphne said. "You're the one that brought her into our life! I heard you on the phone with her once, Richard. And one night I tried to get you to roll over and you whispered out, *Becca,*" Daphne said in imitation of him.

Behind Richard, she could see Becca's face flush with excitement. She'd inadvertently let the woman know she had a place in Richard's life—in his own goddamned bed.

Becca grabbed hold of Richard's wrist and pulled him back while stepping forward. "He's not yours anymore. He said so. He's mine."

Becca shook herself off and ran her fingers through her hair, trying to position herself as the more attractive option. She was pretty, disappointingly so, and even younger than Daphne was. With her hair tousled, her chest heaving with anger, it was so easy to see what Richard loved in her.

"Can we just have a few moments to discuss this privately?" Richard asked Daphne, looking between her and Becca again.

Daphne's eyes widened. "No."

Richard inhaled to protest, but withered under Daphne's gaze. He leaned down to whisper in her ear. "If you let me talk to her alone, I can give the girl some dignity. It'll be easier on us both."

Daphne shook her head. "No." Richard was her talisman. If she was with him, the Master couldn't harass her. "Anything you have to say to her, you can say in front of me."

Becca made an indignant noise for attention. "Look, someone invited me here," Becca said, her voice chilly. "I don't think Richard's that foolish."

"Apparently you've never met my husband," Daphne said, voice just as cold.

Becca took a bold step forward. "If it wasn't him, it was you. What kind of pervert leads someone else on over chat like that?"

"What?"

Richard turned on Daphne, eyes-wide. "Daphne."

"Don't you dare!" she shouted at him.

"I didn't tell her to come here."

"I didn't either!"

"But that's how come you wanted to leave today." Richard looked around the hall at the things she'd packed. "You wanted us to go before she got here."

Daphne blinked. "That's not what happened!"

"Then tell us what happened," Becca demanded.

Daphne whirled on the other woman. "You don't get to order me."

"Let's be rational," Richard said, as if he'd been being so all this time. "It's okay if you told her to come. You were angry, and you wanted her to waste a lot of money, that seems fair."

"But that's—" Daphne began.

"I broke up with George for you," Becca said, louder than Daphne's protest.

Richard stilled, and Daphne could almost physically feel herself losing him, again.

"Richard." She moved to block Becca from his sight, to run her hands up his chest and pull his head down to look at her and only her. "Stay with me. We need to go."

"Good luck leaving," Becca said from behind her. "I had to pay a taxi driver six hundred dollars, cash, to drive me over from the regional airport. He only knew which roads weren't flooded because he'd lived here as a child."

"If there's one, there's others."

Richard shook his head gravely. "I don't have six hundred dollars on me, pet. It can't rain forever."

"But we can't stay here!"

"Why not?" Becca said, and Daphne could hear the hint of triumph in her tone. "This place seems amazing to me."

And then the power, which had been flickering intermittently all morning, went out.

CHAPTER 24

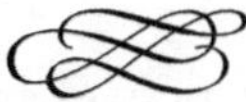

The library was the only place furnished enough to hold the three of them comfortably, with enough windows to let whatever light passed through the storm clouds in. Richard stoked a fresh fire in the fireplace. Arthur or Mrs. Dudley had made a bold effort trying to get Glenn's blood out of the floor that morning, but hadn't entirely succeeded.

Daphne and Becca sat down on opposite ends of the couch, watching Richard stack logs in the fire. When he stood, they both looked at him expectantly, and he frowned. "I need to be alone for a bit."

"No." Daphne protested—none of them should be alone here, in the half-dark, it wasn't safe—

"I just need some space to think." He sliced his hand through the air to cut her off, and stalked down the back hall.

Which left Daphne on the couch with Becca.

Becca stared pensively out the window at the falling rain. Five minutes passed in silence, and then she stood. "I'm going to go look around."

"No," Daphne said again, her voice more stern. "I don't want you alone in my house." It wasn't safe for her to be alone, not when the Master was still here.

"What, are you scared I'll steal things?" Becca glanced up at the Master's portrait. "You think I'll take that out under my coat?"

"It's a big house in the dark. You could get lost."

Becca's eyes narrowed, cat-like. "You really think I'd run from room to room until I found Richard and, I don't know, started blowing him?"

Daphne hadn't considered that until this precise moment, but it seemed all too likely now. "Just like in Paris. Just like in Rome."

Becca's eyes went wide and she flushed. "What—*wait*—that *was* you!"

Daphne clenched her hands into fists at having outed herself. "Just the one time—that was the only time, I swear it—I sure as hell didn't tell you to come here."

Becca's sat back down on the couch and turned towards Daphne. "But the things you said you wanted to do to me...."

"That wasn't me," Daphne said, scooting back.

"Those were why I came out here. Not Paris or Rome. I thought I was seeing Richard's true heart."

Daphne put her elbows on her knees and her head between her hands. Becca was in love with the Master, who she thought was Daphne pretending to be Richard, oh God....

Becca put a hand on Daphne's back. Startled, Daphne looked up, and found Becca's face hovering close—she had just enough time to close her eyes before Becca kissed her.

Daphne jumped back like she'd been shocked, and then sat stock still. Becca's eyes watched her, and she put a hand on her knee, and then leaned in again.

Should I run? Why aren't I running? she thought. But Becca's lips touched hers and it was too late to run all over again.

If she was kissing her, she wouldn't leave, would she? And together they'd both be safe? Yes, that, that could be the reason for this, so that she didn't have to admit to maybe liking it. Daphne opened her lips, and began to kiss Becca back. Her lips were so soft, and her tongue was so gentle, it was like Daphne was kissing a flower. She turned her head so that they could kiss harder, deeper, and Becca made a little noise of satisfaction, before bringing her hand to rest on Daphne's breast. Daphne's breath caught at this, and she felt her nipples rise and she sidled closer so that her knee and thigh brushed up against Becca's and her own hands rose to reach for her waist where Becca's raincoat was tied.

Together they were nearing a hairpin turn, and someone would have to take the wheel and yank it if either of them were going to stop in time, before they rounded the bend together and everything was too late—Becca's tongue sought more of hers out, her lips becoming needy, pulling at Daphne's harder as Daphne's hands deliberately untied the coat.

Fabric fell open, revealing soft skin inside, and absolutely no clothing. Daphne pulled back in surprise, as Becca's hands began to tug her shirt up. Of course, Becca'd done it for Richard—but Daphne got to be the one who took advantage of it. She started touching the other woman as Becca got her shirt free and sent her hands roaming up beneath and lips touched lips again as legs pressed against legs.

Soon they were falling backwards, and Daphne's shirt and bra were off, breasts exposed to Becca's mouth as she stroked her fingers against the other woman's breasts, pinching at her nipples.

"Tell me that you want me."

"Hmmm?" Daphne's voice was soft, entranced by the creature she was touching and all the delicious touches she was getting in return.

"Like you did online."

Her mouth closed and her teeth grit. She'd read the chat logs, she knew exactly what the Master had said—and Becca's hands were going lower now, pushing up beneath her skirt—

Daphne grabbed a hank of Becca's hair near her scalp, twisting the woman's head to the side. "I want you," she said in a low voice, spreading her legs open in invitation. With her other hand she grabbed Becca's tentative one and pulled her higher, forcing her to feel the wetness staining the cotton between her thighs. "See?" she said, more her own voice, less channeling the Master.

Becca's face lit up—and she pulled Daphne's underwear down and off as quickly as she could, then returned to hover over her again, her raincoat covering both of them, to watch Daphne's face as she slid two fingers in.

Daphne gasped and writhed. It was wrong, there should be no room for Becca inside her life, muchless between her legs, but—as the other woman started to move her fingers in and out and pull inside her with her hand—it felt too good to stop.

She reached up and pulled Becca's mouth to hers again, kissing the other woman deep, her wet hair falling down around them both like a curtain. She kissed her as hard as she wanted Becca's hand to fuck her, as good as it felt to be fucked, and she tilted her hips up so that Becca could reach even deeper inside. She began to moan, and her own hands left Becca's breasts to drift down to where Becca's pussy waited, brushing through the small thatch of dark hair to run her fingers against the other woman's folds. Becca's skin down there was as soft as her lips, all the moreso because she was as wet as Daphne, and Daphne felt them curiously, tugging Becca's labia gently.

"Go on. Do it," Becca whispered, her voice hoarse. Daphne slid one finger in to Becca's warm heat, and felt the delicious softness continue, even up inside. Becca shivered, her own hand in Daphne stopping, as Daphne pushed another finger inside of her and began to touch the smoothness that she found there.

It was magical to touch inside another woman, to share her most intimate space. Daphne found herself ignoring the sensations of Becca inside of her, and concentrated on this, the yielding velvet that moved whenever Daphne pressed—and wherever Daphne pressed, Becca moaned, which made everything even more delightful. Soon the other woman pulled her own fingers out and balanced on all fours above Daphne, arching her hips back into Daphne's hand, while Daphne tried to touch more of her, inside and out. Her lips kissed at Becca's neck and her free hand lifted the weight of one of her hanging breasts, and always, always, she was moving her fingers inside, pushing and pulling her hand, sensing all of the ways she pleased Becca as the woman's eyes glazed over and her breath became an endless series of moans.

She felt the velvet of Becca's pussy tighten and redoubled her efforts to reach more, press more, pull more, and then Becca threw her head back and shouted, going still before quaking bodily, making Daphne fight to follow her orgasm as she came, her hips twitching of their own accord, wetness spilling out of her like she was a fountain, dripping down Daphne's hand and forearm.

"Oh God, oh God, oh God," Becca breathed, collapsing down onto Daphne's chest, still shuddering—revealing Richard standing not six feet away, in his robe again, standing over them, watching them with glittering eyes, a cigar in one hand, a snifter of brandy in the other.

"How long have you been there?" Daphne said, trying to get her elbows underneath her.

Becca looked over her shoulder to see him, and then returned her attention to Daphne, moving back to all fours to crouch over her again. "Let him watch."

Before Daphne could protest, Becca's fingers were sliding back inside and the other woman's mouth was on her breast. She didn't want to come, not by Becca's hand in front of Richard like this, but her body needed this, it wanted it, and the monster the Master had made of her craved it—Becca started pulling her nipple in and sucking on it while below her fingers alternated between fucking her and rubbing on her clit, and her voice rose like she wasn't in control of it, an otherworldly cry, louder than the sound of the thunder and the rain—Becca wasn't going to stop until she'd pulled an orgasm out of her and Daphne had one waiting, close, so close—Daphne shouted incoherently, up on her toes, the muscles of her pelvis taut, trying to pull Becca further in.

Becca's last movement—fingers, thumb, tongue—released her. Daphne curved up, body in turns rigid and loose, as the orgasm flowed through her like a wave of the thunder that echoed outdoors.

Richard sat down on the head of the broad couch, and pet her hair, as she gasped for breath. Why was she so easy to own whenever, wherever, sex was concerned?

"And that's why people want to fuck you, pet," he whispered, almost to himself.

$\mathcal{B}$ecca collapsed on top of her, their legs tangled, breasts to chests and arms, and Daphne held her because she didn't know what else to do. Richard continued to pet her hair, in silent contemplation.

"We still have to leave here," she said.

"Now that all the cats are out of the bag—and have been fucking in my library—why should we?" Richard asked.

Becca chuckled, Daphne felt it even if she didn't hear it.

"Because it's dangerous here. I can't explain why, it just is. We need to start over, somewhere else."

"Pet, the power flickered on long enough for me to check the internet. Becca's right, the roads are drenched, and the airport's been shut down." He stroked a thumb along her forehead. "When the storm's over—tomorrow." He lifted the snifter up to his lips and took a sip. "Let's give this place just one more day."

What next? How could she get them to leave now? She could hardly convince either of them of there being a ghost now, not after she and Becca had fucked. She inhaled to try again regardless, but Richard moved his hand to cover her mouth. She let her mouth close and sagged back into the couch, as his fingers traced lines over her face, following her cheekbones gently, the shells of her ears, tugging on her earlobes, the line of her jaw, and then to brush his forefinger against her lips, like he was putting lipstick on her. She was quiet under his ministrations, relaxing—somehow, being in here with the two of them at least felt safe—and then he pressed his finger into her mouth.

She looked up, and saw him looking down, eyes dark. He started fucking her mouth with his finger—just like he was hoping she would soon blow him.

Sex was safer than words were—and if they were together again, she still might be able to convince him to go—he pushed his finger in and out and she sucked on it, hard enough to make him go slower. He set the snifter far away on the ground, giving his full attention to her.

She reached her hand that was around Becca back to touch his chest, and felt him purr. Becca raised her head, looked at him, and then again at Daphne, as if for permission. Daphne didn't say yes…or no. And so Becca reached out and put her hand on Richard's thigh.

Richard stilled at this, his finger deep in Daphne's mouth. She knew what he was thinking—he didn't want to get into trouble, but he could hardly not take the chance to fuck both of them at the same time. Daphne bit his finger lightly to break his thoughts, and he started to free himself, pulling it out and pushing back.

"I'm sorry," he apologized, even though this time, for possibly the first time in his entire life, he had nothing to be sorry for.

"When was the last time you saw her?" Daphne shifted to be out from underneath the other woman.

"Four months," he answered quickly.

She looked to Becca and the other woman nodded.

"You've been without this that whole time?" Daphne asked, folding Richard's robe back, exposing his erection.

Becca nodded, hesitantly. Daphne reached forward and caught her hand into Becca's hair again and the other woman sagged like a kitten caught by the nape. Daphne raised her up and moved her over, so that her mouth hovered above the head of Richard's cock.

Both she and Richard were tense. Was Daphne rubbing their faces in things, like they were bad dogs? Or was she going to set them free?

"I want to watch you suck him."

Becca's eyes darted at Daphne, not believing what she'd heard. But her mouth opened and her head bobbed and she took Richard's cock inside her mouth, and Richard made a quiet strangled sound.

Daphne watched him closely, as he closed his lips and looked tormented, not sure if he should enjoy himself or not, unable to lose himself in the moment, while Becca's lips worked at him—not until Daphne reached over and untied his robe's belt and started kissing down. Then he finally allowed himself to gasp and groan.

The women worked on him together and apart.

CHAPTER 26

As long as he came inside of her—it didn't matter what else happened.

Daphne licked up his shaft as Becca sank to his balls, and Richard wound his hands in their hair, looking down at both of them with his jaw dropped, completely unable to believe his good fortune.

"Oh God," he whispered, as if to himself. "I haven't been this hard since our wedding night, pet. Someone could brush me with a feather now and I'd come, and then I'd still get hard enough again to fuck the both of you."

Daphne took him at his word, and wrapped her mouth around the head of him, sinking down, eyes looking up—as Becca relinquished him to her, turning to kiss at her breasts instead. Daphne made a sound of surprise at the attention, and Richard growled. "That's it, Becs—taste her. Make her happy."

Becca purred, holding one of Daphne's breasts up for her mouth. She sucked in Daphne's nipple and ran her tongue across it, making it light up, as Richard pulled her head down and thrust forward. Daphne could feel his hard cock bending at the back of her throat, he hadn't been exaggerating, and as she brought her hand up between his legs to feel his sack tightening, she knew he was close.

She pulled back. "I want you in me."

He stared down at her with half-lidded eyes. "What my pet wants, she gets."

Daphne looked between the two of them, feeling a flush, no matter everything that they'd already done. She turned herself toward the fire, on all fours, as if presenting herself for mounting, and knew she should feel some vestiges of shame at their intimacy being witnessed. But the dancing firelight revealed Becca's own full lips parted, her nipples hard, and her breathing fast—Becca was turned on, and she was shameless, and her shamelessness gave Daphne strength.

Richard aligned himself behind her and took her in a solid stroke, so hard it made a guttural sound escape her lips. Her fingers clawed into the floor, trying to brace as he pounded in again. It wasn't like him to take her this hard, but maybe having an audience was drawing forbidden urges up in him—he started rhythmically fucking her, his cock hitting spots of her she'd only thought the Master could, and she started to cry out, forgetting that they were being watched—until she felt a hand on hers.

Daphne's eyes blinked open. Becca, kneeling beside her, waiting for permission—and behind her, Richard slowed. Daphne could scent the other woman's heat same as she could scent her own, and while part of her wanted to grind Becca down—she viscerally knew what it was like to feel lonely.

"Get on the couch," she whispered, and Becca leapt up to do so, laying down lengthwise.

"No—turn," Daphne said, moving herself, so that she and Richard were now parallel to the fire, and in front of Becca's knees.

Daphne rose up a little then, without dislodging Richard, putting her hands atop Becca's thighs and then slowly tracing up, just like the Master had done so often to her. Becca gasped and let her legs part readily, pushing herself down so that she was almost laying flat on the wide couch, exposing herself to Daphne.

Daphne had never been with a woman before, before tonight—but keeping everyone here would keep everyone safe—and—she found she longed to know. What would it be like to do to Becca like Richard did to her? Would she also be able to find Becca's secrets? She'd already made the other woman come once—were more orgasms hiding inside of her, waiting to be summoned? She lowered her mouth between Becca's thighs and lapped.

"Oh, pet," Richard growled, reseating himself in her, thrusting anew.

They were like some carnal machine then, the three of them, Richard pounding into her, making her tongue follow his rhythm against Becca, the other woman endlessly moaning on the couch in front of her, winding her fingers in Daphne's hair. Daphne liked the taste of her, and the feeling of it all—she had pride, yes, but there was some glory in being broken down into her components and being used. Between the two of them she didn't have to pretend to be strong, or to convince them to leave, or even fear that she was being left behind, when it was so clear that both of them so desperately needed her—and then Becca's hands clenched in her hair.

"Daphne," the other woman crooned.

Richard answered, "Yes, Becca, *yes*," because she could not, urging the other woman on. He kept up his pace and Becca's thighs tightened, and then she was shuddering beneath Daphne, howling out her name. Becca released Daphne's hair, as Daphne felt Richard's hands at her hips, pushing her forward, pulling himself out. "Climb up her, pet. Get right on top of her." He urged her forward with his hands and hips, Daphne felt his slick cock slide up the cleft of her ass. She did as she was told, awkwardly clambering over the breathless woman beneath her. "Hold her for me Becs. Hold her like you're me."

Becca's arms wound around Daphne in an instant, as Richard arranged her legs, splaying them outside of Becca's, whose were already open wide. "Pet," Richard purred, rocking back. Daphne twisted to see him stroking himself as he contemplated both of them. "All of this time, I thought you were so pure." The firelight played over only half of his face, casting the other half in unknowable shadow.

"You never asked for anything else," Daphne said, lightly frowning. She was turned on, there was a growing ache between her legs that needed to be serviced, and her breasts were pressing against Becca's. If she wriggled, she could feel skin rub skin.

"My dirty girl," he went on. "Becca, what do you think we should do with dirty girls?"

Daphne gasped and looked down, and saw the other woman's eyes go wide with power. "Richard, darling," she said, with a mischievous grin. "Surely we fuck them."

Richard laughed his throaty laugh, the one that she'd fallen in love with, and she felt him come near. "Indeed."

HE WAS on her in an instant and she threw her head back at the feel of it, his cock sliding into her up to its hilt. Becca's hands were wound about her, chest and waist, holding Daphne still for the onslaught of his attention. One of Richard's hands came forward to wind in her hair, as Becca kissed her throat, and Daphne felt trapped, one corner of an unholy trinity, spread wide by her husband's mistress for her husband to fuck.

It was incalculably wrong, and yet compared to what she and the Master had done—she remembered *him* in a flash and wondered if *he* was there with them, in the room tonight, having a private viewing of their very personal orgy.

And then Richard's cock pulled all the way out of her, she felt the head of it almost pop out of her tight pussy and she whined. "Patience, pet," he counseled, and then Daphne felt Becca shift beneath her. Becca cried out, and it was Daphne's turn, suddenly her job to hold the other woman still, as her husband's cock rammed into her.

"Take it," Daphne whispered, then tested out her husband's nickname. "Take it, Becs." If Becca had been with the Master, and the Master had turned her on…. "Let him fuck you like he owns you," Daphne said, because she knew it was what the other woman wanted to hear. Sure enough, Becca whined at that, tensing beneath her, so Daphne went on, in between increasingly savage kisses at her exposed skin. "He's going to fuck you so hard, Becs. So hard you can barely take it," she began—and then it was her getting fucked, Richard had shifted himself again.

Becca kissed her anywhere she could reach, while Richard's cock thrust up, the width of its head rubbing her deep inside. "You both," he grunted, without finishing the thought. "This is amazing," he went on, pulling his cock from Daphne again to shove it into Becca, who moaned below Daphne at the sensation.

Richard's hands grabbed her ass to hold on, pounding wildly, going from Becca's pussy to hers and back again, and Daphne's head was spinning, same as if she were getting spanked, or getting fucked with her waist bent over a leather bench. There was no knowing where Becca was going to kiss her next, or she, her, or how long Richard would thrust for, only how hard, because he was so hard, he hadn't lied earlier, Daphne was sure this was the hardest he'd ever been.

And then he was fucking Becca again, beneath her, and Daphne heard Becca gasp and gulp. "Oh my God," she whispered, words at last instead of moans. "Richard—don't stop," she pleaded.

Richard bent over Daphne's back, breathing down over the both of them. "Never," he growled, and Daphne could feel the heat radiating off of the other woman as she started to spasm below. Becca curled forward, coming hard, hissing and shouting, and while Daphne was turned on, a part of her was horrified, at feeling Richard's thrusts reverberating through the other woman—was she being left behind, again?

And then Richard rammed his cock inside her and pushed any doubts she'd had aside. "Now you, pet," he whispered in her ear as he filled her. She could feel the weight of him over them both, his sweaty chest against her back, and he grabbed her hand, winding her fingers in his own. "I want you to have everything you desire," he said roughly as he covered her. "I'm going to spill myself in you, again and again. I want you dripping with my cum, and I want every other man who sees you to smell me on you and know you for the dirty girl you are."

Something in the moment felt hot—*felt right*—and Daphne cried out, feeling her pussy wrap and grab him. He grunted at that, and thudded harder still. "Yes," he grunted. "*Yes,*" he moaned and hissed, and Daphne knew from the feeling of his cock throbbing inside her and the jerky way his hips spasmed against hers that he was coming, that he'd saved everything up, for her and her alone.

She was his and he was hers, and she hadn't made a mistake marrying him, and they might really be able to figure everything else out, together—or hell, even with Becca, she was too spent from sex to care—just as long as they could *leave this house.*

RICHARD SLID out slowly as she and Becca caught their breath, and the three of them were quiet for quite some time. Daphne couldn't tell what time it was anymore, the sun was falling into dusk through rainclouds. Richard moved himself first to pull his robe back on and put more logs on the fire beneath the Master's portrait. Daphne stared up at it, knowing that he'd seen everything, looking down at them over his snifter, while holding his riding crop—she glanced over to where Richard had left his snifter on the ground.

"No," she whispered.

"Pet?" Richard asked, looking over at her in concern.

Daphne shook her head.

JUST ONE NIGHT. Just one night. All she had to do to get what she wanted was spend one more night. Daphne repeated the phrase to herself like a mantra.

She made them both come with her into the kitchen to get things to eat for dinner, and then took them back to the library, everyone wildly half-dressed, to eat their plates of fruits, meats, and cheese, and was relieved when Richard switched himself back to wine.

"Now what?" Becca asked. Sleeping with the both of them had subtly changed her position with them.

"We wait out the storm," Richard said.

"And then?" she asked.

"We leave here. We can sort everything else out later," Daphne said, sounding sure.

Becca looked between them, hopeful. "How are we going to pass the time until then?"

Richard broke into a sly grin. "I think Daphne has a ghost story to tell us." Daphne made a face and tucked up her knees. "You said this place was haunted, pet. Tell me why," he pressed. She was quiet and he looked at Becca. "A girl died here, you know. She died outside, near the stable, but close enough."

"That's awful—what happened?"

"The real estate agent wouldn't tell me the whole story. Something about her living here happily for many years, and then suddenly wanting to go…it was like the house wouldn't let her leave. Like it would miss her once she was gone."

"Why would anyone ever want to leave here?" Becca asked, looking around the grandiose room.

"Precisely. Why?" Richard smiled at her.

"Because," Daphne began, screwing up her courage. "What if there were a mean ghost here? One that took advantage of women? And he was tormenting that girl, so much so that she had to leave? And when she did, he couldn't handle it and killed her?"

Richard made a contemplative sound. "What if he loved the girl? What if he needed the girl around his cock? What if he wanted to give the girl everything she ever wanted, and take care of all her needs, for the rest of the girl's life?" Daphne's eyes narrowed and her pulse quickened. That didn't sound like Richard to her. "What if he gave her things no one else could? What if he only fucked her because she wanted it? Because she begged him for it, with her ass hitched high?"

"Richard—"

"Say you wanted it, Daphne. Say you needed it all those fucking times," he said, emphasizing the word fucking.

"Stop!" Without thinking, she slapped Richard's face.

Becca caught her hand before she could hit him again, and Richard's hand came up to cup his face, where a handprint was welting.

"What the fuck, Daphne," he said with his own voice, sounding annoyed.

She yanked her arm back from Becca. "You weren't you—you were being cruel."

"If I was, it was only because you made me," Richard said, voice half a growl.

Daphne scooted back, with a frown.

CHAPTER 27

aphne made Becca come with her upstairs to retrieve enough bedding before the sun went down, so that they could all sleep in front of the warmth and light of the fire.

"This place is really kind of creepy," Becca agreed, after the impromptu tour.

Daphne turned to face her. "You have no idea."

Talking was too dangerous, so no one did. They all lay down, Richard between the two women, both of them snuggled up on either side. Daphne didn't think she'd be able to sleep the whole night. The Master was getting bolder—and what if the storm didn't break?

Her concentration was broken by the sound of Becca's contented snores, and she snorted. So did Richard.

She rolled up onto her elbows and looked down at her husband. "What've you gotten us into?"

He shook his head. "I don't even know anymore." His eyes rose up to look at the wall behind her. "Hang on."

He disengaged himself gently from Becca, and Daphne moved out of his way as he stood. He walked over to the portrait and Daphne bit her lips as he took hold of it and started prying it up off the wall.

It fought him—ages of dust probably gluing it down—but he finally lifted it away. There was a terrible stain on the wall behind it, where the paint had rippled because of something—*water? what?*—underneath, and a pervasive musty odor. Richard swung it out and turned it, setting it down so that they could see the back of it, and all the Master could see was books.

"Thank you," Daphne whispered to him.

"The only reason it stayed up there was because you liked it. But I didn't want him staring down at us tonight."

"Me either."

Without the portrait watching, the mood lifted. Daphne looked around at their situation—it was like they were attending a particularly ridiculous slumber party, and she bit back a smile.

"There's my pet," Richard said, settling in on her far side, raising himself up with one arm. Daphne turned towards him.

"It is you, isn't it?" she asked, looking deep into his eyes.

"Who else would it be?"

She swallowed, not wanting to answer him.

He reached out and put a hand on her waist. She was wearing the rumpled clothing she'd put on this morning while packing, that she'd taken off before sex—she hadn't gone back to her room for fresh clothing yet, and was too scared to go by herself.

Thunder boomed, making the windows rattle. "I don't think your tests are going to be delivered today," Richard said.

Daphne shrugged. "That's okay."

"You haven't given up on me, have you?" he asked her. Daphne looked up at him, confused. "You still want a child with me? When you know how badly I've screwed up?"

Daphne licked her lips in thought, then nodded. "Yes."

Richard's countenance changed, she could almost see his whole body relax. "Good." He smiled, pleased as punch, and rocked himself near her, pushing her down and pulling her close.

As he rocked on top of her, Daphne gathered his intent. "But," she said, and cast a glance back at Becca.

"But what? You're my wife." He settled himself inside her. "She's fun—but this is why you'll always be my only," he said, groaning quietly with his first thrust.

"Just me?"

"Just you, pet."

She bit back a gasp as he filled her again. Why did it feel so right? Maybe because now there were no lies between them, and now there was nothing keeping them apart. She felt tender, having weathered his attentions earlier in the night, but being sore made each new thrust somehow more satisfying. He wanted her once, he wanted her twice, he'd keep wanting her forever.

Their sex was furtive, like high schoolers worried about getting caught, seeking solace instead of satisfaction. But when he was in her, and he was himself, Daphne felt like a weight was lifted, and that there was finally a light at the end of her very long tunnel. They could leave here tomorrow, drive away, drop Becca off or take her with them, she honestly didn't care anymore, as long as they had each other and they were not here, they had the rest of their lives to figure everything out.

They rocked there, their hips matched, their mouths open as they breathed short breaths. They were both trying to be quiet—despite the martial rights they had with one another, oddly neither wanted to be rude. But an orgasm was building inside her, she could feel it winding up, like the twist of an explosive fuse. All she needed were a few more strokes to light it and—her hands clawed into his shoulders as she hissed her orgasm out, and seconds later she was filled with his cum for the second time that night. Richard lay on top of her, as if staking a flag on a new mountain, claiming all the space she occupied for him.

"We fit so perfectly," he whispered in wonder, before falling to one side.

. . .

Daphne fell asleep feeling safe in Richard's arms—and because of that, she was surprised when she woke up alone.

"Richard?" The fire was low, and the rain was over, the only illumination was moonlight trickling in from the high windows above—and Becca was nowhere to be seen, either. "Becca?"

She stood up. Why was she alone? "Richard!" She shouted his name at the top of her lungs, listened hard for a response and heard the sound of a distant smack. "Richard?"

Another blow. Daphne's breath caught in her throat, and she ran upstairs to the old four-poster bed.

"Richard! Becca!" she shouted, her voice raw with terror. She reached the upper hallway and then heard the sound of blows, louder and more frequent.

Daphne drew up to a stop in the hallway, looking into the room. There were no curtains and the moon was on this side of the house, letting bright-white light in, casting an otherworldly glow over both of their bodies. Becca was crouched on the bed, tied to the two posters nearest Daphne, her ass in the air on her knees, with Richard standing behind her, head bowed in concentration, the crop she'd rescued from the stable in one raised hand.

Becca looked up, gasped in shock at seeing Daphne there, but Richard didn't stop his blow.

"Richard—don't!" He looked up and over at her. His face changed, emotions cast over it, twisting it strangely, making it look like it belonged to someone else. "Oh no." Daphne put a hand to her mouth and pulled back into the darker hallway.

"Daphne—wait," Richard said, his voice not his own, like he couldn't use his lips. She watched him take two steps and he was awkward like an automaton, like someone who didn't remember how to walk inside a body. "Stop!" he shouted after her, his voice deeper and laced with gravel.

Daphne whirled and raced down the hall.

.   .   .

"DAPHNE!" The Master's voice coming out of Richard's mouth, making the words misshapen and horrible, like he couldn't work Richard's lungs or lips. She heard him stumble against the stairs. "Daphne!"

She ran barefoot across the entry hall and back upstairs to the bedroom. Where were Richard's keys? It wasn't raining now, she was going to take the goddamned car and leave. She tossed Richard's bedside table, and his lamp fell to the ground, rattling. She caught it with both hands. "Shh!"

"Daphne!" He was closer now—he'd see her if she ran out of the room again—where could she go? "I only want to be with you, Daphne!" the voice that wasn't Richard's shouted from right outside the door.

Daphne bit back a scream and lunged across the room, reaching for her closet door. With the things she'd packed earlier gone there was room inside for her—she crouched down and tried to calm her breathing.

"Where are you, Daphne?" The Master's voice, slow and rough, like Richard had had a stroke and eaten cotton. "I need you," he said, making the 'u' into a howl.

She kicked her feet out, trying to get further away from him, and felt her back against the closet's back wall—and then felt it give behind her. She fell back and only barely stopped herself from screaming.

She crawled back into the darkness and closed the door, because that was what it was, behind her. She heard him open the closet door and reach back and try the door—of course he knew it was there, of course—and she held it shut as though it were latched. She thought her heart was going to explode—*how could he not hear it?*—but he stopped, closed the closet door, and moved on.

Daphne sagged. Whatever she was on right now felt like concrete or stone. Would he come back? If he did, she couldn't be here—she slid her hands out, and found the edges of what felt like stairs.

She crawled down the stairs on all fours, until she reached what seemed like the ground. She stood—this place smelled like damp and dust and rot—she reached out, trying to find a wall and hopefully a light-switch.

Instead a pull-string batted her in the face. She screamed, swatted it away, and then finally realized what it was and yanked on it, not expecting anything to happen. But they must have repaired the power over night—a naked light bulb flickered overhead and she slowly turned around.

This was the dungeon. The place the Master had talked about with Becca—and where he'd brought her that one intense night.

It was cold. The floor was stone and the cracked leather furniture was covered in dust. The thing he'd bent her over was in the center of the room, it looked like a gymnast's horse, and there were stains around it on the floor. She jumped back so as not to touch any of them—and then realized they were symbols. They formed a massive circle around the horse—and when she knelt down to see if she could read them, she realized they were painted in blood.

Whose? And how long ago? Had they been here when the Master had fucked her? She turned to look for other exits—and saw a pair of work boots behind a cross.

No. It couldn't be—she didn't want it to be—but she had to know. Screwing her courage up, she crossed the floor, a hand ready to cover her eyes—and spotted Luke's corpse on the floor. He was the reason for the smell—and all the blood was his.

"Oh god." Daphne fell down, cupping a hand to her mouth in horror. She thought he'd escaped, and instead the Master had lured him down here for his perverse ceremony.

Daphne's stomach dropped. She needed another way out.

THERE WERE stairs at the far end of the room and she ran to them as if she were being chased and raced up, only pausing to listen before opening the door, before emerging into another, empty, closet. She sat there for a moment, trying not to pant. There was every chance Richard would be waiting for her on the other side.

What if it really was him again? If the Master left him alone?

It didn't matter. It was too late—she couldn't trust him anymore, not until they were free.

She steeled her will and opened up the door and found herself alone in the green room that she'd been thinking of using for her nursery. The girl's photo was still on the ground, glowing in the moonlight. She picked it up and now could clearly see the thing behind girl and her trophy looming—and knew it was the Master.

She put the photo down and crept out into the hall.

WITHOUT KEYS, she was stranded. But Theo's phone number was down on the telephone stand. She tip-toed down, listening wildly, and carefully picked up the phone. Theo's business card, with her cell phone number, peeked out from underneath Richard's note taking ledger.

"Hello?"

"Theo—it's Daphne."

"What time is it?"

"I need you to come and pick me up. Please. I have to get away."

"It's three in the morning—"

"Everything your aunt told you was true. This place is haunted—I'm begging you, please, come get me."

"Okay, okay," Theo said.

"Don't come inside the house. Just honk when you get outside and I'll come out."

"You're twenty minutes away. More with this weather—"

"It doesn't matter. You just have to come. I'll be outside, waiting." Daphne wished she'd had the presence of mind to pick up better shoes while she'd been inside her own damn closet. Had she tried to pack any earlier on? Fuck, fuck—

"Be safe—but hurry, please."

"I will."

Daphne carefully and quietly hung the phone up.

. . .

SHE SANK down and trotted down the hall. The house was too big, the Master could be anywhere—all she had to do was get outside.

"Richard!"

Becca's voice—still from upstairs. Daphne put her hand on the door handle.

"Goddammit! Come back here, Richard!"

Could she just leave Becca alone here, with him? She didn't love the other woman, but no one deserved that fate.

Daphne waited, then pulled her hand back with a curse, and turned towards the second floor.

SHE KNEW it could be a trap. Richard could be waiting right outside for her to come. But after what'd happened to Luke—she went slower, but she didn't stop.

When she reached the room, she looked inside. Becca was thrashing on the bed, hands still tied.

"Shh," Daphne said, running into the room once she saw it was empty.

"What's going on? What'd you do to him?"

Daphne worked at Becca's knots. "That wasn't him—"

"What are you saying?"

"He's possessed." She freed Becca's first wrist, keeping an eye on the door. Becca started laughing at her.

"He's right. You are insane."

"How can you not notice how he's talking right now?"

"He's drunk is all. We woke up while you were sleeping and had a few and then he wanted to do all this to me." Daphne freed her other hand so she grabbed and shook the rope. "It was just like he said online—"

"I thought that was me?" Daphne helped the other woman off the bed. She was drunk too and shaky.

"One of you. You're both fucked up." Becca swayed, and Daphne caught her.

"It doesn't matter now, we need to leave."

"I'm not fucking leaving—"

"Yes, you are." Daphne started to drag her out of the room.

"Richard!" Becca shouted at the top of her lungs—and Daphne heard stumbling footsteps coming up the stairs again.

Daphne yanked Becca towards the door—being caught in the hallway would be slightly better than being caught in a room.

RICHARD HAD REACHED the top stair by the time they were free. If they rushed him now, could they push him down the stairs together? But what if it killed Richard, and not the Master?

"Richard—you're still in there, I know it. You remember me." She held Becca back, as the other woman struggled. "You don't want to hurt us. You can push him out and be yourself again, Richard. It doesn't have to be like this."

His hands clutched at the railing, and she thought he was fighting for himself. "Please—Richard, you've got to try. For me. For us. For our baby."

Richard thrashed, his whole body doing a herky-jerky dance, like he was on fire. It distracted Daphne for half a second—long enough for Becca to break free.

"She's the one that untied me. I was willing to wait for you." Becca clung to his side, pointing to Daphne in accusation. "I didn't want to leave—I wanted to stay here with you."

Richard stilled again, and when he next spoke Daphne knew the battle had been lost. "You will," the Master moaned, with Richard's mouth.

"Really?" Becca sounded impossibly hopeful. The statues at the top of the stair behind Richard watched everything, implacable.

"I don't want her," he said, in seeming response. But Daphne could still see his face by the moonlight and knew the Master was talking to her, not Becca. She watched him bring his arms up, higher than they ought to be for a hug, and she knew what he was about to do.

"Don't!" she screamed, as he broke Becca's neck.

"I only want you," he moaned.

She flew past him for the stairs and he lumbered after her.

DAPHNE REACHED the front door and getting out of the house felt like resurfacing from a sinking boat—she took huge gulps of air, like she'd never tasted it before. Then she started trotting down the stairs and towards the main driveway.

The road was open and the trees were low—Richard would be able to see precisely where she was and come for her. She could out run him, but for how long?

Then Daphne saw lightning strike a tall tree. It lit up the pre-dawn dark, sizzling down, Daphne could hear it, and the smell of ozone cut through the air like a knife. Thunder rumbled so loud she almost dropped to her knees.

It was like the sky itself was chasing her back inside—she couldn't run down the driveway now, exposed to the elements and to Richard.

The only other place she could think of to go was the stable.

DAPHNE TOOK off her heels once she reached grass and raced along one of the many paths that Luke had tended. Luke—*poor Luke*—he was dead because of her. Because the house had turned her into some crazy beast in heat for anyone—tears streaked down her face as she ran, terrified and ashamed.

She reached the stable and huddled inside of it, finally protected from the rain. She'd hear Theo's horn and run out and reach the car before he did somehow and Theo would take her away from here— she could come back with police and sort everything out under the safe bright light of day.

A branch broke nearby—and she heard the shuffle of an unsteady foot being dragged through mud.

She stepped back into the darkness of the stable as Richard appeared.

"Pet," he croaked with a voice not his own. "I know you're in here."

Daphne held her breath as her heart raced. He lumbered in. "I can smell your pussy, pet. Ready for me, again."

She took another step back—and kicked a rake, betraying her. His head tilted and he took two more steps into the darkness with her. Lightning flashed close behind him, and she threw up an arm against the light.

"Richard—please—stop this—"

"There's no Richard in here anymore." He took another step forward, closing the gap between them. He spoke with slurred deliberation. Daphne swallowed—and ran for the stairs to the workshop.

He was faster now—as she reached the top stair, he grabbed hold of her ankle and almost dragged her down, but she kicked free. She scrabbled out onto the workshop's wooden floor, feeling splinters shove inside her hands, as she got to her feet, and Richard came up through the door. Water dripped through the ceiling in places, and moonlight shone through wide cracks.

"There's no where you can run, pet." He lumbered to standing, blocking her only route of escape.

"How are you doing this?"

The Master chuckled. "I am as willful in death as I was in life. I only needed blood, sex, and an opportune form to become whole."

Daphne looked around for exits. There was a rope hanging from the ceiling, perhaps it brought a ladder to an attic down.

"What—what happened to the girl?" Maybe if she could make him talk, she could buy herself time.

"For years she was too young, and then, when she was old enough, she rebuked me."

"And that's why you killed her?"

"No. Her horse did. I merely went to say hello, and it spilled her and all her brains," he said his voice dark and taunting.

"That's awful—"

"Is it?" he pressed. "Is it worse than being trapped here, watching people live lives that I cannot for decades?"

Every other word he moved closer to her, and she moved back, like they were dancing.

"Why me?" Daphne asked, her voice rising in fear.

"I had given up hope, until I saw you, Daphne, or rather the imprint of you in this foolish man's mind. You're the kind of woman that needs fucking, that craves it. You were wasted on him. You wouldn't be on me." His voice became smoother as his control of Richard improved, and he flashed her a wicked smile. "Do you know what you do to men? What it's like being in the same room as you? No man sees you and doesn't wonder how you taste, how you smell, envision your legs around his waist and his cock thrust deep. A woman like you comes along once in a century, pet. I should know."

The workshop table was at her back. There was no place else to hide.

"All I need to do is fuck you one last time as him, and this body will be mine."

Daphne took a deep inhale. This was her superpower. It was the reason her mother had kept her locked inside for her own protection, like a modern day Rapunzel, and—on some level—why Richard had hidden her away out here. People who met her wanted her—and then they didn't want to share. "Okay." She hopped up onto the workshop table, feeling the sharp tips of rusty woodworking tools poke against her thighs. She pulled up her skirt, and felt in control again. "Take me."

"Yes," the Master said, his voice a hiss. He opened Richard's robe, revealing the erection pushing out.

She squirmed backwards, as if afraid. "Be gentle."

"That's not what you want, pet—and we both know it." He brought himself up to the front of the table, and grabbed her hips to pull her towards him. He was staring down, looking for the moment when his cock would enter her and seal his devil's deal—which was why he didn't see her grab up an awl and plunge it into Richard's right ear.

The Master made an unholy sound, swatting at her hand, as Daphne scooted back again, knocking tools to the side as she skittered on crab legs down the table and away from him, hopping off at its far end to run for the rope hanging down. Two tugs like she was ringing a giant bell, and the dusty ladder to the roof fell down. She scampered up it and through a small trap door to stand on top of the stable, exposed to the storm.

CHAPTER 28

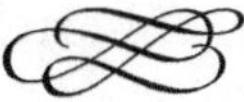

$\mathcal{D}$aphne huddled down, bare feet and knees scraping against the rough wet shingles, trying to hang on. She saw a hand appear at the edge of the hole behind her with horror, as the Master hauled himself up, the awl still poking out of one ear.

"I'm so sorry Richard. This is all my fault—I'm so sorry!" she shouted at him, hoping her husband could somehow hear her.

"Did you think you could kill me?" The Master said, pulling himself to stand on the roof's flat center. He took three more steps towards her as she scooted back, looking over her shoulder. Soon, death would be her only escape, just as it'd been the girl's.

"Come here and let me fuck you," he crooned, blood spilling out of his ear and down the side of his neck.

Daphne stood, trying to swallow down the bile of her fear and praying for strength. "I give up. I'll come back with you." She patted the air between them as if attempting to calm a rabid dog. "You've won."

Richard stood straight, triumphant—and she looked over her shoulder one last time. The fall would kill her, wouldn't it? But if it did, *would she be trapped here, forever, with him?*

Thunder boomed just as lightning struck. Daphne screamed at the

191

nearness of the sound, as the roof beneath both of them shook like an earthquake. She whirled—and saw lightning hitting Richard, the tallest thing for miles, sparks shooting away from the awl in his ear. He danced like a spastic marionette until the lightning was done and he crumpled down to slide off the roof.

Daphne crawled over, profile low, and tried to see him. She was sure Richard was dead now—but how did you kill a ghost?

In the distance, she heard a car horn honk.

DAPHNE RAN on shaking legs back to the ladder and then down the stairs and out the stable's door. It was on the other side of Richard's body—she didn't want to see what the Master had done to him—and she raced through the woods again until she reached the front of the house, where Theo was standing on the porch, about to knock on the door.

"Don't!" Daphne shouted.

Theo turned, saw her, and jumped. "Daphne? Are you okay?"

Daphne caught the other woman's arms. "Don't knock. Don't let it know you're here—take us away." She pulled Theo towards her car and reached for the passenger door handle.

"What the hell happened to you?" Theo asked, turning the engine over as Daphne fumbled with her seatbelt. The engine coughed, once, twice, but the finally took, and she sagged.

"Just drive—I'll tell you everything later."

"Okay." Theo took them around the roundabout and then back down the driveway.

"Faster—"

"It's raining—"

"Faster!" Daphne pleaded, and Theo pushed the gas pedal down.

The car sent up tails of water from puddles in the driveway's worn ruts, and Daphne could see the gates coming up—they just had to reach them in time, before the Master tried to drag them back. Theo slowed down to take the final turn onto the main road—and the car was full of a sensation of heat, as though it were being cupped by the hand of an angry god.

"It's too late for you, Daphne!" The Master's voice rang inside her head. Theo hit the gas again and the car strained forward, but the rear fishtailed as though someone were trying to hold it back.

"What the?" Theo wondered.

"Go! Go!" Daphne shouted, covering her ears with both hands, trying to keep the Master's voice out. He was laughing now, an awful sound, and it echoed inside of her head—then the car broke loose and leapt through the gates.

"Oh my God," Daphne said, reacting to the sudden silence. She twisted to look back, and saw a dark figure standing just inside the metal bars, the same one that was visible in the picture of the poor horse-girl. "We're free. Take me to the nearest police station, please."

"What the hell happened?" Theo asked.

Daphne inhaled. How could she ever explain things? Luke and Becca and Richard were dead—would the police make her go back? She couldn't. If she ever went back, the Master would never let her leave—

The bile rose in her stomach until it couldn't be denied. She rolled down the window and barely leaned out of it in time, puking outside, and then sagged back into the car.

"I'm so sorry," she blotted her lips with the back of one hand.

"Don't be," Theo said. "It's still raining—it'll wash off." She looked over at Daphne with fresh concern. "Are you pregnant?"

Daphne blanched, put both hands to her stomach, and knew with the certainty that some women get that she was.

"Yes," she said, her voice shaky and cracking.

Richard's?

Luke's?

"Congratulations," Theo said, looking Daphne over again. "Right?"

His?

"Right," Daphne said in a quiet voice, entirely unsure.

I HOPE you enjoyed Rough Ghost Lover! Keep reading for a sneak peek at Blood of the Pack, the first book in my Dark Ink Tattoo series, a sultry, sizzling dark paranormal set in Vegas!

For more about my other book, playlists, and cat photos, sign up for my mailing list by clicking on the word HERE or go to http://www.cassiealexander.com/roughghost-news

BLOOD OF THE PACK: Dark Ink Tattoo Book One
   Cassie Alexander

I HEARD an engine turn the corner, startled, and the MMA fighter I was touching up a truly regrettable tribal tattoo on yelped.

"Sorry. Spine," I apologized, peeking over his hulking shoulder to see Jack Stone arrive on time for work, possibly for the first time ever while in my employ. His black 1963 Lincoln Continental swooped through Dark Ink's parking lot like a hearse.

Just Jack. I knew what his car sounded like. Even though our shifts didn't overlap often – I'd heard it often enough to know it wasn't a bike. And still….

I sprayed my client's shoulder with cool water and wiped the blood away, trying to ignore the slight jitter in my hand. This was my job – this was my tattoo-shop – and I'd been doing tats for the past seven years in peace. I breathed deep and willed myself calm. I wasn't scared and I hadn't lost control, and if I kept telling myself that long enough eventually I might believe it.

I put the heel of my hand on the fighter's back to steady it and stepped on the pedal to get the gun roaring again, starting where I'd left off, cleaning up some cheaper artist's shoddy job. In no other profession was the phrase 'you get what you pay for' so true.

This time, the fighter twitched, not me. No way not to hit nerves when you were tattooing someone over bone. Tattoos on top of bone felt like you were getting stabbed.

A lot like getting menacing letters from your ex in prison.

FIVE MINUTES LATER, Jack was leaning over from the wrong side of the counter, purring my name. "Angela."

I didn't turn around. I knew where he was, of course, I'd just made it a habit to ignore him. Mostly.

"Hey, boss-lady, I'm on time, just like you asked," he tried again. I snorted, stopped working, and looked up.

A gaggle of barely-old-enough-to-be-in-the-shop girls flocked behind him, flipping through flash displays, clearly whispering to themselves about him. He was stare-worthy. If you were into tall, lean but muscular men, black hair, brown eyes, and full sleeve tattoos, Jack was your kind of guy. When our shifts overlapped I had to remind myself he was off limits the same way that ex-smokers have to remind themselves to forget about cigarettes. I knew it was for my own good – I'd quit men that were bad for me a long time ago – but that didn't make it any less hard.

It was also why I tried to ignore him. It was good for him sometimes.

"On time for once," I corrected him.

"It's winter," he said, like that was an explanation.

I saw the post office truck pull into the parking lot behind him and my stomach clenched. "Yeah, of course," I said without thinking, standing and pulling my gloves off. "Wrap him up, will you?" I said, sidling towards the hip-high swinging saloon door that divided our half of the shop from the client's.

"My pleasure," Jack said, setting his ass down on the piercing display case and spinning his legs over to switch sides. Normally I'd yell at him about that, but – I reached the door just as the postman did, opening it up to take our letters from him.

Junk mail, tattoo convention flyers, the electricity bill and – something stamped 'Approved by the LVMPD'.

Goddammit.

I bit my lips and ran for the office. I stopped myself from slamming the door, just barely, instead whirling to place my back against it, like that would help keep all the monsters at bay, and slowly sank to the floor.

I threw the rest of the mail to the ground and opened up Gray's letter.

Visit me.

Funny how it only took two words to blow my life apart. I bit the side of my hand to stop from screaming – but somewhere on the inside, a hidden part of me howled.

I tore his letter up – same as I'd torn the other three I'd gotten, starting two weeks ago, and threw the pieces of it into the trash. If only escaping Gray were so easy. I should've left years ago – given myself and Rabbit a head start – but then what? Keep running forever? When I knew Gray and the Pack would always be able to find us? No, instead I'd pretended that I'd had a normal life – that I was normal. I'd rolled the dice, praying that someone meaner and nastier than Gray would take him out in prison.

I should've known that no such person existed.

I'd lived in Vegas my whole life – you'd think by now I'd be a better gambler.

There was a quiet knock on the door behind me. "Boss-lady?" Jack's voice, full of concern.

I stood and straightened myself out, opening the door a crack. "I, uh, didn't know what to charge him – so I asked for two-fifty. That enough?" Jack asked.

It was way more than I'd have asked for. It was only a touch up, hadn't even taken an hour. "He paid that?"

"I can be very convincing," he said, and shrugged, searching what he could see of me with his expressive eyes.

"Stop that. If I wanted to tell you about it, I would."

He leaned forward and pressed the door open. I could've fought back – could've closed the door – but I didn't want to make a scene. But my office was meant for only one person, one desk, one chair, there was no way for us be in here and not be in one another's space. In other circumstances I'd thought about doing things to Jack in here that'd make even the most jaded local blush, but now – I'd much rather he hold me and lie to me that everything was going to be all right.

"What was that?" he said, jerking his chin at the other mail still littering the floor.

"Nothing."

He stared me down. Could he really read me? Or was he just one of those guys who made you think they could? The kind you had relationships with where you filled all the silences with too much hope?

"Seriously, Ang," he said, his voice low.

I gestured to include the entire parlor. "It all says it's for me."

"Even the one from the Las Vegas Metropolitan police department?" he asked. "Don't ask me how I know what stamped mail from prison looks like."

Damn, Jack being Jack. Too smart for his own good. "It's none of your business," I said, as boss-like as I could, shutting down the conversation.

Jack took his cue. "All right, all right,"

"And I need to go."

"Yeah, to your date, I know."

I hadn't told him I was going on a date tonight, that that was why I needed him to really-I-mean-it be on time for once. And he'd said it with almost precisely flat inflection, so I couldn't really tell if he was jealous or whatever – and it didn't matter, because I was with Mark now, anyhow. But some deep and secret part of me bared its teeth and wagged its tail.

He glanced down at the letters. "If anything bad comes of that, you let me know, okay?"

"Sure," I lied, and pushed past him, out the door.

Keep reading Blood of the Pack: Dark Ink Tattoo Book One – and just in case you missed the chance the first time, if you'd like to join Cassie's mailing list, click here or go to http://www.cassiealexander. com/newsletter – to find out about more books and secret scenes!

<u>Bloodshifted</u>

The House—a find your fantasy erotica

<u>The House</u>

Her Future Vampire Lover—futuristic vampire paranormal romance

<u>Her Future Vampire Lover</u>

Her Ex-boyfriend's Werewolf Lover—a sexy paranormal romance

<u>Her Ex-boyfriend's Werewolf Lover</u>

Rough Ghost Lover—a sizzling erotic horror—DOES NOT HAVE HEA

<u>Rough Ghost Lover</u>